PROHIBITION THE NOBLE EXPERIMENT

A STORY OF THE

GREAT PROHIBITION

A HISTORIC NOVEL

ROBB FELDER

PROHIBITION

This story is dedicated in loving memory

of

Joe and Alice

Who gave us all

a home in the brewery

also

Andrew and Anna

Frank, Lewis, Henry,

Catherine

and

Rose

ROBB FELDER

This is a story of The Great Prohibition.

January 16, 1920 to December 15, 1933

This is the story of a brewery and of the pioneer family that ran the brewery.

This is the story of how the great Prohibition of the 1920s ended the life of this brewery, and how the Fellerer family struggled to reopen the brewery at Perham, Minnesota.

This story is based on fact and contains actual historic events.

PROLOGUE

1919

It was a cold and blustery December day in Washington, D.C. in 1917. A young Senator from Minnesota made his way from his office in the Senate Office Building to the Capitol. In his briefcase he carried his final draft of a new bill. There were twelve hundred pages of it. The bill had already passed Committee, and he would submit it to the House for a vote. When it passed there, it would be forwarded to the full Senate for a majority vote.

The bill would have his name on it. He was Andrew Volstead, Senator from Minnesota's 10th Congressional district in the town of Granite Falls. This bill, when passed, would forbid the manufacture, distribution, and sale of all alcoholic beverages in the United States.

The bill passed both the House and the Senate by December 18, 1917. It was then sent to President Woodrow Wilson for signing, however, the signing was postponed because of World War One. President Wilson instead issued an executive order prohibiting the sale of grain for the manufacture of alcoholic beverages because of the war. However, most manufactures of alcoholic beverages had already stockpiled enough grain to get them through the war.

In 1919 The President signed the bill, which became known as the Volstead Act. It then had to be ratified by three fourths of the states. After the ratification by 36 states, the bill became the 18th amendment to the constitution.

On January 16th, 1920 Prohibition began- - - - .

THE BREWERY

The original brewery at Perham was founded by the Northern Pacific Steam Brewing Company in about the late 1860's or early 1870's. It was located at a place on the west bank of the Ottertail River where the Northern Pacific Railroad had surveyed for the place where the new railroad would come through from Duluth, through the towns of Brainerd and the town of Staples, and cross the Ottertail River at Perham, before proceeding westward and across the Perham Prairie and on into the Dakota Territory. The brewery was built to accommodate the lumberjack crews cutting timber around and north of the Big Pine Lake area, and the crews of 'river drivers' who floated logs down the Ottertail River to the Clark and McClure saw mill which was located next to the brewery, at the falls, and to saw mills further downstream, to the saw mill at Ottertail City, and to Fort Abercrombie on the Red River.

A fire destroyed the brewery in the late 1870's, Peter Schroeder bought the brewery property in 1879. He rebuilt the brewery and expanded the brewery building brew house and the cellars. He built a new malting operation with a malting floor and a new malt dry kiln. The barley grain for the malt was grown all around the Perham Prairie by the farmers who settled there, even before the new town of Perham was started.

THE BREWMASTER

Andrew Fellerer was born in Sulzbach, Bavaria, Germany in 1860 and came to America in 1879. Anna (Munstadt) Fellerer, his wife, was born in Hamburg, Germany in 1868 and came to America in 1884.

Andrew came from a family of brewers in Germany. Andrew's Father, Frank Fellerer owned and operated his father's brewery in Sulzbach, Germany. Andrew worked at the family brewery until his father's death and the brewery was sold. He then left for America. In Milwaukee, he attended a brew master's school and worked at the Pabst brewery.

Joe Fellerer was Andrew Fellerer's eldest son. He was a 4th generation brewer.

The Noble Experiment

Prohibition; - - - How did this happen?

It was President Hoover who coined the phrase: ***"The Noble Experiment"***.

The Eighteenth Amendment to the U.S. Constitution went into effect on January 16, 1920. It wiped out the beer, the breweries, the saloons and the culture that had come to define the American social life.

We look back on this Noble Experiment called Prohibition today and we can't quite understand how that could have happened. What were people thinking? Ironically, things weren't that much different back then, than they are today in a number of ways: Economic turmoil, corporate greed, a widening gap between the rich and the poor, an unprecedented expansion in the brewing industry, immigration issues, scandal-filled news headlines, a middle class worried about the direction of the country.

It sounds like today's headlines, but these were the same problems facing American society at the turn of the 20th century.

Over the last few decades of the 1800's; rapid industrialization and unprecedented immigration in America created a country of big cities and booming growth. Many reforms were instituted in the early years of the twentieth century - - - the eight hour work day and forty hour work week, labor unions, child labor laws, minimum wages, most importantly; Women's Suffrage, guaranteed by the 19th Amendment. On June 4th, 1919, the U.S. Senate passed the 19th Amendment.

But, all of this prosperity and reform had a definite dark side - - - - - -.

With more disposable income and free time, the American workers were looking for more pleasurable pastimes.

Sometimes, it is hard for us to imagine life at the turn of the 20th century. Our standard of living has advanced so far and so fast. It's hard to imagine life without all the new inventions and technology that we enjoy today.

Imagine, if you dare, to consider life; before the advent of the automobile, radio, movies, television, cell phones, space travel, computers, or the internet. The main escape and social outlet for the working class was found in the saloons. That's right; saloons, they were everywhere, often four or five on the same block. They were the "social-media" of the times.

Aside from newspapers, saloons were the only medium available for the discussion of the current issues and local news.

This bears repeating; - - -

Aside from newspapers, saloons were the only medium available for the discussion of the current issues and local news.

Gambling and prostitution were frequently associated with these establishments. But the largest problem was the consumption of alcohol. By the turn of the 20th century, the per-capita consumption of booze had risen to about 20 to 40 gallons of liquor per person, per year.

If you do the math on those statistics; with approx. 10.66 of the 12oz. glasses in each gallon, that's about 213 to as much as 426 glasses, or cans of beer per year, per person.

POWERFUL WOMEN
AND
SLEEPING BREWERS

There were a number of factors that led the US down the path to Prohibition. The most important factor was the rise of powerful well organized and well-funded organizations whose sole purpose was the elimination of alcohol.

The two most prominent organizations were the WCTU (Women's Christian Temperance Union) and the ASL (Anti-saloon League). In a time of growing and changing society, these groups saw alcohol as the primary factor in the degradation of society - - particularly in the cities.

Over the period of about 40 years, beginning in the late 1800's, these groups worked to affect public opinion and elect local politicians who helped work to turn their counties dry. They worked to eventually elect congressman who supported their cause. Because of their efforts, by late 1914, it was estimated that about 50% of Americans were already living under total Prohibition.

Another major factor was that the brewers were asleep. They didn't see Prohibition as a significant threat and so they mounted almost no opposition. Taxes collected on beer, wine and spirits; (with beer by far the largest contributor) made up about 20 to 40% of the federal government's income. The brewers just assumed that neither the people nor the government would ever be able to give up that revenue.

Game Changer

But then, a different Amendment changed the game entirely. In 1913, Congress passed the 16th Amendment, introducing the **Income Tax,** and suddenly brewers were vulnerable. Alcohol tax revenue was no longer necessary for the government to function.

Game Over

The 65th Congress convened in January 1917, in which the "dries" outnumbered the "wets" by 140 to 64 in the Democratic Party, and 138 to 62 among Republicans, thanks largely to the efforts of the WCTU and the ASL. When America declared war against Germany in April 1917, German-Americans were a major force against Prohibition. Many of these prominent German brewers of the day- - -were widely discredited because of the war with Germany and their protests were subsequently ignored.

HOW IT ALL BEGAN

THE WHISPERING SNOW

1887

Whispering, "It's whispering to me," Anna thought, "Snow whispers when it comes down in the woods." The snow began falling, lightly at first, but was coming down at a pretty good rate now. "It doesn't whisper like this in the city," she thought, "not in the city of Hamburg, Germany, where I grew up, and not in Milwaukee, Wisconsin, the first city I had lived in when I first came to America. But here in the wilderness, in the big White Pine country of Minnesota, with no city sounds to distract it, the snow whispers as it falls." There was only silence at first, before the snow, then as the snow started, lightly at first, then harder, and with not even a breeze, the snow began to whisper as it fell through the tall pine trees. You can only hear it after you've experienced the sheer and utter silence of the big pine woods. This was Anna's first winter in Minnesota and she had heard about how snowy and cold it could get here. They, she and Andrew, had already experienced several light snowfalls, in November starting back about the first of November. But they had come with a lot of wind and blowing snow, but not a lot of heavy snow. Now on December first, Andrew had said, "this looks like it's going to be a very big snow." He had already readied the sled by moving the box from their wagon onto the bunkers of the sled. This sled had four heavy skis, and like the wagon, the first two attached to the tongue that was hitched to the team of horses, and swiveled just like the front wheels of the wagon. The back set of skis was stationary.

Andrew had purchased the homestead rights to 160 acres in 1885, after he had secured a position at the Schroeder's Brewery at Perham as the Maltster. Andrew then acquired a team of horses and a wagon. He also bought the necessary tools to cut enough timber to build a log house, and a barn for the horses, and cleared some of the land and made a road into it.

In Minnesota, in the late 1880's, the logging industry in this part of the state was at its peak. The new Indian treaty of 1867 had opened up a great part of the vast White Pine forests of northern Minnesota for logging. Timber rights were easily obtained by logging companies. This was followed by new settlers obtaining homestead acres. Some homesteads were on 'clear-cut' land ready to be 'opened up' for farming. Some homesteads on the prairies were basically ready to be farmed. Some homesteads still had large stands of virgin white pine. Andrew's homestead had large stands of this virgin white pine.

He had just arrived from Milwaukee. He came by train through Duluth and then on the new Northern Pacific Railroad to Perham. He had left behind, temporarily, his new Fraulein in Milwaukee, Anna Munstadt, who was also an immigrant; where they met, and fell in love, and where he had graduated from a brew masters school and had worked at the Pabst Brewery in Milwaukee. After Andrew had secured the homestead and completed building the log home and barn, he wrote a letter to

Anna, inviting her to join him. When she arrived in Perham, Andrew proposed to her. They were married in the town of Perham, Minnesota on April 14, 1887 and moved into the new homestead. Andrew was 27 years old and Anna was 19 years old.

****

Very early that morning Andrew had hitched up his team of horses to the sled. Just before he left for work with the sled, he had said to Anna, "are you sure you'll be okay here till I get back from work?"

"Oh, I'll be fine," Anna reassured him. I've been feeling just great ever since I got past all that morning sickness, back when I first got pregnant, and I know this is the first of December, my due date, but I haven't felt any contractions yet."

"Ok," Andrew said, I'll try not to worry, but you know Mrs. Herman, your midwife said you could have the baby right at her house, and she lives close to the brewery."

"No, I want to stay home and have the baby here," Anna replied, as she kissed him good-by. She then said, "Just be sure to bring Gretchen Herman home with you. I know, I feel fine so far, but I really don't want to go through this alone. And, drive carefully Andrew, especially on that bad curve by the lake. It's snowing pretty good already." They had talked to Gretchen earlier and she said she would be available. She and her husband, Carl lived close to the brewery where he also worked as the cellar manager. Andrew then left for the day saying, over his shoulder "I'll try to get off early Anna, Mein Frau, I love you."

Later, about mid-morning, Anna walked through the snow, the 'whispering snow', to the horse barn, a short distance from the house, to feed her horse, a young mare that she had named Caroline, after her mother. As she walked along in the new, falling, "whispering" snow she was having a feeling of euphoria as the snowflakes danced thru the trees and down upon her. She began to dance with the falling, whispering snowflakes as she tilted her head back and let the snowflakes lite ever so briefly on her outstretched tongue, just as she had done as a little child, recounting how very special and lucky she felt right now in her life. She was going to become a mother. She had always wanted to be a mother. She absolutely loved children. She was married to a man that she loved, and was someday going to be a very successful Brew Master of the brewery at Perham, she began thinking again, about her mother, back in Hamburg, Germany. She missed her so much.   She thought of her mother very often. And now as she walked through the deepening snow, she also began thinking of her brothers and sisters too, especially her older sister, Martha, her favorite of her siblings. If the baby would be a girl, she and Andrew had agreed they would name her Martha. If the baby would be a boy, they would, of course name him Joseph, after Andrew's older brother.

These young pioneers, Andrew and Anna, like most immigrant pioneers, missed their families a lot. These courageous immigrants left behind their families and their homeland and ventured out into the utter unknown. They had no idea what lay ahead. This was the ultimate adventure. Their stories would be different for each one of them in this vast new land. The only connection they had with the families they left behind was the mail. The mail to Europe in the 1800's took about a month to get there, so about two months to get a reply back from someone. They would write a lot of letters back and forth whenever possible. Anna was thinking of this as she walked through the snow. She had written letters to her mother and her sister Martha, as well as Andrew's family, telling them that she was pregnant and expecting their first child the first of December.

Her sister Martha wrote back, "We are all so excited for you and Andrew. We can't wait to hear from you when the baby is born. I do so wish that I could be with you for this. You write the minute that baby is born."

Anna arrived at the barn and as she came through the door, her mare Caroline whinnied at her. She ran up to her and petted and nuzzled her, petting her nose and cheeks. The horse was a gift from Andrew, a wedding gift, to give her freedom and mobility while he was away at work, at the brewery, about 12 miles away. She loved her horse, and every time she rode her she would think of her mother. But now, her Caroline was also pregnant, and could not be ridden. She would have her foal in the spring. They had bred Anna's mare because they decided that they would need another horse for a second team if they decided to start logging off the timber on their homestead at some point in the future. She then grabbed the pitch fork and loaded some hay into Caroline's manger. Next, she grabbed the wooden bucket next to the stall and pumped it full of water from the pump in the corner of the barn, and brought it back and set it down on the floor of Caroline's stall. She watched her drink until she was full, then removed the bucket. She went over to the grain barrel and picked up the grain scoop, and as she bent over and reached down into the barrel for the grain, she felt this horrific cramp grab her entire lower abdomen and lower back and she practically sunk to her knees. She gasped and had to hang onto the edge of the grain barrel. The cramp continued for almost a minute, then it passed. This was her first experience with this of course. She had no idea what to expect, and no idea what was yet to come. At last she was able to pick up the grain scoop and fill it from the barrel and carry it over to Caroline's grain box. She patted Carolina's snout for a second and thought, "I'd better get back to the house. I don't want to have my baby in the barn, and I don't want to cramp again and go down outside in the snow." Anna was a very strong woman, and tall, almost taller than Andrew, but she now knew that childbirth was going to challenge even her strong constitution. She walked as rapidly as possible back to the house. The snow was coming down harder now, and the wind was picking up. The snow was no longer whispering to her, it was making small swirls in the yard, and the wind was blowing the snow down from the treetops, and she wondered if Andrew and Gretchen would be leaving the brewery soon for home. She got into the house and lit the kerosene lamp on the mantel. The skies were darkening rapidly even though it was still mid-day, as the snow was coming down heavier than ever. She found her favorite book and stoked the fireplace, and got into her rocking chair near the lamp and fire. She thought, "I may as well read to keep my mind off of this until Andrew and Gretchen arrive home. I hope I don't have another cramp until they get here."

****

The original brewery at Perham was founded by the Northern Pacific Steam Brewing Company in about the late 1860's or early 1870's. It was located at a place on the west bank of the Ottertail River where the Northern Pacific Railroad had surveyed for the place where the new railroad would come through from Duluth, through the towns of Brainerd and the town of Staples, and cross the Ottertail River at Perham, before proceeding westward and across the Perham Prairie. The brewery was built to accommodate the lumberjack crews cutting timber around and north of the White Pine Lake area, and the crews of 'river drivers' who floated logs down the Ottertail River to the Clark and McClure saw mill which was located next to the brewery, at the falls, and to saw mills further downstream, to the saw mill at Ottertail City, and to Fort Abercrombie on the Red River. A fire destroyed the brewery in the late 1870's, and Peter Schroeder bought the brewery property in 1879. He rebuilt the brewery and expanded the building and the cellars. He built a new malting operation with a malting floor and a new malt dry kiln. The barley grain for the malt was grown all around the Perham Prairie by the farmers who settled there, even before the new town of Perham was started.

****

Andrew opened the valve and let the steam into the steam engine which powered the grain elevator to bring the last of the daily batch of malt from the malting floor in the basement, up to the top floor of the malt dry kiln. He then climbed the stairs up to the top floor of the kiln. The kilning floor was a floor made up of heavy steel mesh screening. Here he would spread the malt out across this screen floor to be dried, as it came up from the basement malting floor. The screen floor was an area about twenty by twenty feet square. The malt was quite damp yet, where it had lain and sprouted on the floor of the basement with frequent watering, this sprouted barley was called malt.

He reached the kilning floor and walked over to the spout of the malt elevator where it came down through the roof from the head of the elevator shaft. He then 'rapped' with his shovel three times to signal to his assistant, Jim Schmidt in the basement to begin shoveling the malt from the floor into the mouth of the elevator. Soon the damp malt began pouring out of the chute. As Andrew began spreading the malt out across the screen floor, he could feel the heat rising up from down below, where earlier he had fired up the kilning furnace, which would dry and lightly roast the malt in two separate phases. After spreading the batch out to a depth of about two inches, it was then left for about two hours to dry for the first phase. Andrew then went back down to the main floor and checked on the furnace and stoked it again with just the right amount of wood to dry, but not scorch the malt. He then went over to a window to check on the storm.

As Andrew stared out the window at the falling snow, he began to think about his brother Joseph back in Milwaukee. He had left their home in

Sulzbach, Germany, and came to America ahead of him and went to Milwaukee to pursue a career in the brewing industry. Joseph had already secured a job at the Pabst brewery when Andrew got to Milwaukee. Both of the Fellerer brothers had worked at their father's brewery in Sulzbach until their father died and the brewery was sold. Andrew began reminiscing how good it had been to see Joseph, who offered Andrew a place to stay in Milwaukee while he attended brewing school, and later as Andrew looked for a job, at Pabst, and at other breweries in Milwaukee and other large cities of the Midwest. It was then that Andrew had met Anna Munstadt, and began dating her, and fell in love with her. Then finally he got the offer for the malting position here at the Schroeder brewery, in Perham, Minnesota.

He still felt apprehensive, and guilty about leaving Anna alone this close to her due date. The snow was coming down pretty good now, so he went outside to his team of horses and got the horse blankets out of the box on the sled and covered the horses with the blankets so they wouldn't get wet and cold. He came back in and went down to the basement to help his assistant Jim, clean up the malting floor for the next batch, although there wouldn't be a new batch for a while. They swept up all of the old malt left behind from previous batches and threw it out. They then hosed down the floor, because that was the last batch they would do until after the holidays. The current brewing season was just about over and Andrew had done double batches of malt each day for the last week or so, so he could take time off to be with Anna and the new baby. The malt bins were now full, and the lager tanks in the cellars were now full of beer as well, and this would last through the holidays. Typically, the winter months after the holidays were the slow season, where the demand for beer dropped off until spring. So they brewed only every couple of days until about March when the new brewing season would begin again.

With the malting floor now cleaned up, it was about noon and time for lunch. He and Jim went upstairs to the lunch room where several other brewery workers were already gathered. The two keg washers and the two keg fillers where there. Heinric, the keg manager remarked, "I think we'll be knocking off early today. With this snow storm really picking up out there, our drivers aren't going to be making any afternoon pickups or deliveries."

Just then Karl, the cellar manager came in, and as he saw Andrew, said to him, "I'm surprised you're still here. I'd have thought you'd be leaving already. You've got quite a ways to go, and Gretchen's been packed up, and ready to go since this morning."

"I know," Andrew replied, "I'll be leaving as soon as I finish up my batch of malt. It's on the kiln floor now and will be ready soon to be recycled into the roasting cycle."

Just then Peter Schroeder walked in with a large pitcher of beer for his crew, as he usually did for lunch, and remarked, "Isn't this some fine looking beer. Now that we have a maltster that knows what he's doing, our beer has improved markedly." As he spotted Andrew, he said to him, "good job, Andrew. Your malt batches are very consistent and roasted to perfection for our lager. By the way Andrew, you should be leaving now because of the storm."

Andrew then replied, "I still have to run the last batch through the roasting cycle."

Peter then told him, "Why don't you have Jim finish up the roast cycle, so you can get on the road."

"Hell no," retorted Andrew, "I have to do it myself. The temperature has to be just right, and I can tell when it's done by the color and smell of it. It only takes an hour, then, I'll hit the road."

Peter then replied, "Ok, Andrew. Have a safe ride home. Give my best to Anna. I hope she has a good delivery."

As Andrew and Jim hurried back to the kiln, Andrew said to Jim, "that talk back there has made me very nervous, let's hurry and get this batch finished up so we can both get home." They hurried up to the kilning floor where they used long handled scrapers to rake, or pull the malt into holes in the floor where it fell into a large hopper, where it was then elevated back up to the kilning floor and again spread out, for the roasting phase. The purpose of this recirculation of the malt was to break up any clumps from the drying and to reposition the malt on the screening floor for the roasting phase. After the malt was spread out, Andrew went down and again stoked the furnace to a higher heat to lightly roast the malt. While they waited for the batch to finish, they went over to the brew house and started up the malt crusher, and ran a previous batch of malt through the crusher, and elevated it up to a hopper above the mash tub where it was ready for the next brew. That took about an hour. They then hurried back to the kiln floor where Andrew tested the malt for color and smell. "It's done," Andrew exclaimed, "I'll let you finish up now, getting this batch off the floor and elevated over to the malt storage bin. I'm getting on the road. I'll see you in about a week."

"Okay," Jim replied, "good luck getting home, and good luck to Anna with the baby."

Andrew ran out to his sleigh and quickly uncovered his horses and folded and stored the blankets. He then ran the team about a half mile up the road to the Herman house. He knocked and Gretchen answered. She was also nervous and apprehensive as she said, "here grab my suitcase and we better get going, the storm is worsening." It was about two P.M. and as they raced down the road to where it crossed the Northern Pacific Railroad tracks, they discovered a train stopped at the crossing that had been heading north. The locomotive was right at the crossing, and the engineer shouted to them, "It's going to be a while. I have to wait for the southbound train to pull onto the siding in Perham so I can go by. They said the tracks are snow-blocked west of Fargo. I will probably only get as far as Fargo tonight with this storm, then wait for the plow. They said this whole line will be closed with drifting snow by morning." Andrew and Gretchen had to wait for almost an hour for the train to move. As they again took off down the road, Gretchen said to Andrew, "This is not good. Now it's probably after three P.M. It will probably be after dark before we get to your house."

Andrew was becoming more worried now and he put the horses into a fast trot. He didn't want to gallop them yet. They still had a long way to go. The road went straight east for about five miles before turning north to go around the north side of White Pine Lake. where it curved sharply and headed east again past the logging camp where the loggers dumped logs into the lake to be boomed down the Ottertail River, in the spring, past the brewery to the sawmill just south of the brewery. The road then went about another five miles to Andrew and Anna's homestead.

LOST IN THE STORM

They rode along in silence for a long time, each of them becoming more tense as the twilight slowly turned more and more into darkness, and the snow kept swirling across the road. Driving a team of horses at night was a bit treacherous in itself, but it was even more so on a slippery, snow-covered road in the dark, in a blizzard. They had to rely more on the horse's instincts for staying on the road than their own. As they came to where the road turned to go up and around the lake, Gretchen warned Andrew, "please be especially careful at top of the hill where the road makes that sharp right turn to go east. It's at the edge of a cliff with about a 30 foot drop into the lake."

"I know," Andrew retorted, "that curve is dangerous enough in the daylight. I'll try to take it slow and easy at the curve." But as the road climbed up and around the lake, the wind came howling across the lake carrying with it a ton of snow, drifting across the road and creating a complete and total 'white-out'. Even worse, when they got to the top where the road curved sharply, there was a drift about 4 feet high across the road. As the horses scrambled to get over it and pull the sled thru as well, they started stumbling and slipping, and losing their footing in the slippery snow. As they stumbled and scrambled in the total white-out, they momentarily lost their direction. They got too close to the edge and the horse on the left started slipping over the edge of the cliff. This started the sled sliding over the edge, Gretchen gasped, as Andrew grasped the reins tighter. As the horses found footing again, they pulled back up onto the road, this caused the sled to suddenly turn and become perpendicular to the road. This sharp change of direction caused the skidding sled to drop halfway over the edge of the cliff. As it skidded along the edge, it caught on a patch of bare ground, swept clean by the high wind, causing the sled along with Andrew and Gretchen to tip half over, dumping them both over the edge of the cliff. Gretchen screamed, and Andrew yelled out, their voices swallowed up by the howling wind and the driving snow. They tumbled head over heels down the side of the cliff, yelling and screaming all the way down. Lucky for them, first of all, the deep snow cushioned their tumble, and secondly, the brush on the side of the cliff slowed their descent, and thirdly, the lake at the bottom of their tumble was already frozen over, so they didn't end up in the water. They were extremely grateful for all three, and expressed their gratitude to their Creator for all three, as they scrambled around trying to find each other in the total darkness and white-out.

* * * * * *

Anna woke up with a start and looked around. It was already dark outside. She must have dozed off for a while after reading for most of the afternoon. "I'd better get supper started," she thought, "they will be getting home soon." She went over to the kitchen area and lit another lamp, and started a fire in the cook stove, then got out two frypans off the shelf by the stove. She went to the ice box and got out a ham and sliced off several slices and put them into one of the frying pans. She put the rest of the ham back in the icebox. As the stove heated up, she got several potatoes from the bin in the corner. These were potatoes from her garden, from last summer, that she was so proud of. She peeled and sliced the potatoes into the other frypan after she put in some bacon grease from the lard crock in the cupboard, and just a dab in the ham pan. This was Andrew's favorite supper and she loved making it for him. Tonight she made extra because they were having a house guest for several days. As the ham and potatoes sizzled in the pans, she looked at the clock on the mantle. It was about five o'clock. She went over to wind it. She normally reset it at sundown, but no sun today, so she just wound it. In a few minutes, the ham and fried potatoes were done, so she put them into the oven to stay warm, and she also put in some biscuits and bread to warm up, until Andrew and Gretchen got home, and then she set the table. Earlier she had another contraction, but it wasn't as intense as the first one, and she thought, "these are really far apart yet, I must have a really long way to go." So she grabbed and lit a lantern and headed out into the snow, to the barn, to feed Caroline her supper.

* * * * * *

Gretchen wanted to find her suitcase and climb back up to the road. But Andrew said, "No", to both ideas. He had to yell to her over the howling wind, "We'll never find it in the dark and white-out. We'll have to come back and look for it after the storm, and the hill is way too slippery to climb up from here. I think what we need to do is go out onto the lake to get out of these huge drifts along the shore and go back along the shore to the base of the hill where the road is low to the lake, and take the road back up to the curve, and if the sled isn't damaged too badly we'll be in luck."

So that is what they did. It was slow walking on the lake, and the snow was almost a foot deep, but better going when they got onto the road and discovered that when they had come through earlier, the horses and sled had left a trail, on the road, up the hill thru the snow. When they got to the top they had to scramble through a now five foot high drift. They stayed next to the woods side of the road this time, in the total darkness. They were very paranoid after going over the cliff. When they got through the drift, they expected to find the team of horses and the sled, but there was no sign of them or the sled. They didn't really want to feel around and stumble around in the black dark and white-out at the edge of that cliff. The wind was howling so bad, they couldn't even talk to each other by shouting. So Andrew grabbed Gretchen's hand and led her along the edge of the road using the brush for a guide. When they got around the curve, the trees protected them from the wind, and they could talk again. Andrew spoke first, "I think the team of horses took off after the sled tipped and dumped us. Without anyone at the reins to stop them they would just keep going, and we can't even see any tracks, it's snowing so hard"

"Maybe," added Gretchen, "they went to the logging camp. They probably smelled other horses."

"I agree." replied Andrew, "the logging camp road is just a little way up on the left. We can get the team and sled and get back on the road. We'll be home in time for supper. I'll bet Anna is getting worried about us. I sure am worried about her, all alone when the baby is due. I've done nothing but worry about her all day." "Don't worry too much about Anna," Gretchen reassured him, "she's a very strong girl, and besides, the first baby is always late."

After they found the logging road and turned down it, they walked along in silence for quite a while, keeping to the edge of the road with the brush guiding them on the right. They couldn't actually even see the brush in the total black darkness and swirling snow, they had to let it brush up against them for direction. After about an hour they stopped to rest and Gretchen said to Andrew, "shouldn't we be getting there by now?"

Andrew replied, "Oh, I don't know, pushing through this knee-deep snow is pretty slow going. Let's keep pushing on some more." So they went on some more in silence, and in about another half hour they stopped again and Gretchen said,

"This can't be right, I just know we should have been there by now."

Andrew replied, "I now agree, I think we should have too. Maybe we somehow wandered off the main camp road in this blackness. The road does seem narrower than before. Let's go a little further though, and see if we can see the lights from the camp." So they walked on some more. About another 20 minutes later, they stopped again.

Andrew then said, "This can't be the road to the camp. This is way too narrow. It's become more like a trail."

Then Gretchen replied, "I would certainly agree. We must have wandered off the main camp road in this blizzard. I think we've become lost. We could be in big trouble without any protection from this storm, and it's starting to get colder. But wait, isn't that a faint light I see in the distance, through the trees?"

They pushed on some more, toward the light, then, stopped. Andrew said, "Wait, isn't that a campfire? I don't think the loggers would be outside by a campfire. They would be inside having supper by lamplight."

Just then they heard a horse whinny, and a dog started barking. They moved closer and came to a small clearing where the campfire was burning and lighting up the area. On the other side of the fire they saw three Indian teepees. Just then the flap of one of the teepees opened and an older Indian man stepped out to see why the dog was barking.   "Who are you, and what are you doing at our camp on a night like this?" he questioned, speaking in the Chippewa language. Gretchen because she was an older person, understood some Chippewa language and replied, but in English, "we were looking for the logging camp, but wandered off the road."

"We lost our team of horses and sled", Andrew continued, "When we fell down the cliff back on the main road by the lake. The horses didn't go over the edge, but they just took off. We think they went to the logging camp."

"I know the place", the Old Indian replied, "Very dangerous place."

Andrew then remarked to the old Indian, "Shouldn't you be on the reservation?"

"No", replied the old Indian, "we are allowed to take the fish we need from these lakes for the winter as stated in the treaty of 1855, So we come early in the winter and set up this fishing camp and fish through the ice when the lake first freezes. We will be leaving soon, we almost have enough fish for the winter. We also come here in the fall to harvest wild rice on the lakes and down the Ottertail River as far as the brewery and sawmill. The other two teepees are my sons and their squaws and children. But why don't you come into my teepee and have something to eat. You look tired and hungry. We have fresh fish from the lake."

"Thank you," They both replied, as they all entered the teepee. When they were inside, the Indian said, "My name is Billy White Wolf, and this is my squaw, Silver Wolf." Andrew replied, "I'm Andrew and this is Gretchen."

"Your squaw then?" Billy asked.

"No," Andrew replied, "Gretchen is a mid-wife. I was taking her home with me. My wife is expecting a baby anytime now, and I'm very worried about her, home alone. We really must be going. Can you show us the way to the logging camp?"

"No, no, not tonight", Billy White Wolf replied, "no one should be out in this storm. We could all get lost. We'll go first thing in the morning." Then Silver Wolf spoke up, "come, sit and eat", she said, "we still have some fish and wild rice bread left, and Mr. Andrew, you don't worry so much about your wife. The great spirit takes care of a woman bringing new life into our world."

* * * * * *

Anna was getting worried, very worried. The supper was getting cold, and there was no sign of Andrew and Gretchen. The storm was raging outside. "Where could they be?" she thought, "are they still on the road, stuck in the snow?" she wondered, "or, maybe Andrew decided to stay at the brewery for the night. Or, maybe they are holed up down at the logging camp."

* * * * * *

Andrew and Gretchen sat and started to eat as Billy asked, "So where do you live Andrew?"

Andrew answered, "My wife Anna and I have a homestead about four miles east of here, and I work at the brewery."

"How about you Gretchen", Billy then asked her.

"I live near the brewery, and my husband also works at the brewery", she replied. By the time Andrew and Gretchen finished eating, it was getting late. Silver Wolf began laying out some blankets on the floor of the teepee for Gretchen and also for Andrew to sleep on. Billy White Wolf went over to the side of the teepee and brought out a small keg of beer and said, "let's have some of this 'spirit water' from your brewery. Silver Wolf and I usually have some every night. It helps us fall asleep. We traded for this, down at the logging camp. We traded a side of venison for it. Some of our young sons get a little crazy from it, but my squaw and I just use it to put us to sleep, except it makes me get up to pee several times during the night.”

So they all had several cups of the 'spirit water'. The fire was dying down by then, so they all laid down on their blanket beds. First Billy went over to a pile of blankets and pulled out two large beaver blankets and gave one each to Gretchen and Andrew. “You'll need these, it's going to get cold in here by morning when the fire dies down”, he said.   'I trapped these beaver up on your homestead before you bought it.”

“I do remember there being a large dam and beaver lodge on the creek that flows through the homestead”, Andrew said.   They all fell asleep quickly with plenty of 'spirit water' in their bellies.

* * * * * *

Anna was becoming frantic with worry. The supper was now cold. “Where could they possibly be”, she thought.   “Are they frozen to death somewhere along the road? Will my baby be an orphan even before it's born?” She began pacing the floor. She went into the bedroom and checked again, the baby's crib, and the new baby's clothes that she had made, along with several baby blankets, and a couple dozen diapers. She felt like she was pretty well ready for this baby. Outside, the wind was screaming and howling. Inside, Anna began to have another contraction. This one was even harder than the last. She got into her night gown and crawled into bed thinking "I'd better be in bed, if these cramps continue, I could have this baby by morning." But she only tossed and turned trying to get comfortable with her huge belly. "I just want to have this baby so I can get some sleep", she thought as she climbed back out of bed. She went back out to the living room and relit the lamp and stoked up the fire, and got into her chair by the fireplace and put her feet up on the footstool, and began reading again. She looked at the mantle clock. It was nearly midnight.

* * * * *

Andrew and Gretchen woke up in the morning just as the sun came up, to find Billy White Wolf and

Silver Wolf had already had the fire roaring and she had already made some corn bread. So they ate the corn bread, along with some venison jerky. Billy White Wolf then said, "Well we better get going. It isn't really that far to the logging camp, but Silver Wolf and I, and our family want to get an early start down to the lake and finish up our fishing for the winter." As they stepped outside, the sun was out, and the storm had passed, but it was bitter cold. Probably well below zero. There were 'sun dogs', (Frozen moisture in the air that picked up the sunlight and reflected it in a circle around the sun) They immediately began hiking through the now waist deep snow. Billy knew the trail very well, in spite of the deep snow, and he was right, it wasn't very far to the camp. They walked for about half hour through the area with no trees where the loggers had already clear-cut, and skidded the logs down to the lake and onto the ice where they were piled up and would wait until the spring melt. As they hiked toward the logging camp, the trail went along the lake, and they began to hear the thunder from the lake. Andrew was puzzled, and asked Billy, "What is that noise?"

Billy explained, "In winter, the ice on these lakes here in northern Minnesota begins to crack when it gets extremely cold, like this morning. The ice expands as it freezes, and on a huge body of water like a large lake, when it is extremely cold, the ice will freeze so fast that the ice will begin splitting open as it expands. It will pop open with a very loud noise that sounds like thunder when it echoes off the shore and trees. Then as the crack travels out across the lake, the cracking gives off a sort of moaning sound. Some cracks will go on for miles across the lake. So the ice on a lake is never a solid sheet of ice, but thousands of small pieces. The cracks will then 'heal' themselves shortly by re-freezing the water that rises up into the cracks."

They soon arrived at the logging camp, which was now coming to life. As they proceeded to the office, Billy White Wolf said to them, "We'll leave you now and get back to our fishing. Good luck to you. I hope you find your team of horses and sled." Andrew and Gretchen both said, at the same time, "Thank you so, so much for letting us stay in your teepee last night." Gretchen then said to Silver Wolf, "And thank you for sharing your food with us." Andrew then added, to Billy, "We'll always be grateful to you and your squaw, Silver Wolf. You saved our lives last night by having that campfire burning. I don't know what we would have done if we hadn't spotted it. We may have frozen to death in that blizzard. We are city people and don't know how to survive in the woods, let alone in the middle of a blizzard."

Billy then said, as he and Silver Wolf turned to go, "This woods is the only home we know in this life. And the white man is destroying our home." They then departed, and Andrew and Gretchen went into the office.

They approached the logging crew manager and asked if anyone had seen a runaway team of horses and sled come into camp last night. They then had to explain their misadventure of the night before. The crew manager said, "You two were very lucky. We had a driver of ours, a few years back who got a little drunk on some of your beer and went over the edge at night, horse, wagon and all. It was summer, so there was no snow to cushion their fall down the cliff. He hit the rocks down below, along with his horses and wagon. All were killed. What a mess, we had to pull the whole mess back up the hill, and bury them all. Well, let's go ask around, and see if anyone has seen your sled and team of runaways. You were also lucky to stumble on that Indian camp. They come to their camp often, to fish and hunt, very nice folks. We trade with them often." They then all went outside and began asking around, if anyone had seen the runaways. No one had seen them. Finally the manager said to Andrew "you know what I think happened. Your runaway team stayed out on the main road and ran all the way back to your place."

"You know, I think you're right," Andrew exclaimed, "could I borrow a team and a sleigh from your camp so we can get home. I'm really worried now about Anna. What if she had seen the empty sled and horses come home. She'd be out of her mind with worry by now."

"Tell ya what, I'll send one of my team drivers to get you two home," the manager said, "but it's going to cost you."

Andrew then said, "I'll pay anything, let's just get going. How about you stop by the brewery, and I'll see that you get a couple of kegs of free beer." "That'll be great," the manager responded, as he flagged down a driver with a team and sled. "We're running low on the stuff and this crew runs on beer, especially in the winter months. It keeps them warm and energized all day."

"It's a deal, then," Andrew said as he and Gretchen got on board the sled. "I should be coming by in several days to take Gretchen home. You can follow me in to the brewery." In about an hour they were home, after plowing through the deep snow.

When they got home, the driver turned around in the yard and said, "See ya in a few days. Good luck with the baby, hope everything is alright." They jumped off the sled and ran into the house forgetting all about the lost team and sled. Which, as suspected, had returned the previous night, and because the barn door was open, went right in, sled and all. It was still early morning and the cabin was still dark and cold inside. The lamp had burned down and gone out. They almost panicked when they saw Anna all slumped down in the rocking chair. But she woke up when she heard them stomp the snow off their boots. "Where have you been", she yelled at them. As Andrew ran over to her and she got up, he threw his arms around her. "I've been so worried about you," he said.

"You've been worried!" she exclaimed, "I made a big supper for you guys, but you never made it home. I was going insane with worry about you. I couldn't even sleep in our bed last night. I finally fell asleep in my chair. That was such a terrible blizzard we had. I could only imagine you freezing to death somewhere. I've had nightmares all night long."

"Oh, it's all my fault," Andrew confessed. "If I hadn't been so pig-headed about leaving work, we could have been home before the storm got so bad. I didn't think the storm was going to move in so quickly."

Anna then asked, "Well, where on earth did you two spend the night? Were you at the brewery, or at the logging camp?"

"I'll let Gretchen tell you all about it", Andrew said, "I'm going out to try and find my horses."

"What?" Anna exclaimed.

Gretchen then said to Anna, "why don't you sit down while I explain everything." As she went into the kitchen area to fix Anna some breakfast, Andrew got on his coat, hat and boots and gloves and went back out to look for his lost sled and team. He found them as he walked to the barn. Just as the logging crew manager had suspected, the horses came right back to the barn. He climbed onto the sled and grabbed the reins and pulled back on them, backing the sled out of the barn. He parked the sled in front of the barn, and unhitched the horses and led them into the barn where he took off their harnesses. He put them into their stalls and gave them water, hay and some grain. He did the same for Caroline, Anna's horse. He noticed the feed barrel was getting low so he made a mental note to get a few more sacks of grain from the brewery, when he took Gretchen home in a few days. He then closed the barn doors and walked back to the house thinking, "I'm so grateful that my horses are ok, but I'm still worried about Anna. I still haven't heard how she is feeling." When he got into the house and took off his coat and boots, hat and mittens, Anna came over to him and said, "So, you spent the night with the Indians? Slept in a teepee? And you two could have been killed, going over that cliff! I always worry about you on that curve. Then you get lost in the blizzard. Andrew Fellerer, I swear, you are a crazy man! You should have stayed at the brewery, or better yet, left earlier, and aren't Indians supposed to be dangerous?"

"I know, I know Anna, I'm really sorry for worrying you", he said apologetically, "but I just had to get home with Gretchen, your mid-wife. I have been so worried you would have to have the baby all alone. And no, these Indian people are very good people, Anna. They saved our lives, and took us in from the storm and fed us, and I will always be grateful to them, and respect them for that. They don't deserve the bad treatment that they get from us white Europeans, who are stealing their homeland away from them. But, I'm still worried about you. Are you ok?"

Anna replied, "Of course I'm ok, for now. As I told Gretchen, I had a very bad contraction yesterday as I was out feeding Caroline, but I came in and sat down for a while. Then I had a milder one about mid-day yesterday, and a strong one last night, probably because I was so worried about you. But I haven't had any since, and the baby is moving again. Gretchen tells me those were probable false labor pains, and it could be a while yet. So relax, Andrew, we will just have to wait some more." Gretchen mentioned that she suddenly remembered her suitcase at the bottom of the cliff. She said, "But, we shouldn't go searching for it yet. Maybe I can borrow some of Anna's things, if it's ok with her. We can go looking for the suitcase after the baby gets here."

"Yes of course", Anna replied, and we can always wash out some of your 'under-things' whenever you need to."

So they all waited and relaxed as the rest of the day went by slowly. It was a bright, sunny day, but very cold, although the sun melted a little snow off of the edges of the roof. Andrew busied himself by chopping and bringing in more firewood. They had a big supper. Anna again fixed Andrew's favorite, ham and fried potatoes. After supper they played some cards by lamplight, and they all went to bed early. They slept really soundly after the stresses and anxiety of the previous day and night. They awoke early on December third at sunrise, and as Andrew was returning from the outhouse, he noticed a change in the air. It felt warmer, but very damp. And the sun came up like a big red ball as it turned the eastern sky red-orange, as a cloud bank moved in from the west. When he got back into the house he recited an old German axiom to the girls, "Take warning of a red – red morning." They had breakfast and as Andrew and Anna went out to the barn to feed the horses, it was already snowing. Big 'whispering' flakes, as Anna now called them. By noon it was coming down really hard, and the wind was picking up again as well. Andrew remarked, "Looks like we're in for another snow storm." And Gretchen replied, "This could be what does it."

Anna stated, "I hope so, I just want to get this over. I just want to hold my baby." Sure, enough, by early afternoon, Anna started having contractions again. Real ones this time, Gretchen could tell, because they were long and hard, and at regular intervals, about an hour apart at first. Then at supper time she got up to go eat and her 'water' broke. She got so excited, she decided to skip supper. Gretchen asked Anna if she wanted to get into bed yet. Anna said, "No, not yet."

Gretchen said, "That's ok, you'll know when you're ready." The contractions kept getting stronger and closer together, and about midnight, Anna said, "Ok, I think I'm ready for the bed." Gretchen helped her get undressed and into a nightgown, and into bed. Andrew stayed out in the living room, he didn't want to distract Anna, he was just too tense. A little while later, the contractions were getting real close together and almost unbearable.

Gretchen told Anna, "Don't hold your breath, breathe in little short puffs, kinda like a dog panting."

A few minutes later, Gretchen said, "The head is coming through now, so you will have to push with each contraction. Come on now, push hard. I see shoulders, push."

Anna gave a loud scream, and out came a brand new life into the world. Gretchen held up the new baby, and firmly smacked him on his bottom and the baby began screaming and breathing.

Gretchen said, "It's a boy, Anna."

She laid the new baby boy on Anna's chest while she tied off the umbilical cord and cut it off. She proceeded to clean up the baby and Anna's bottom with a hot, sterilized wash cloth.

Anna yelled to Andrew, "Andrew, we have a boy."

Gretchen took the baby and put a diaper and a pair of pajamas on him, and wrapped him up snuggly in a very soft blanket and returned him to Anna, then covered them both with the sheet and blanket. Gretchen went to the door and opened it and said,

"Andrew, come on in and meet your son."

He went in and Anna handed him their new son and said, "Andrew, we have a Joseph." Andrew took his new son and said, in a very soft voice, "Joseph, welcome to the world."

And thusly began the life story of Joe Fellerer, born on December 4th, 1887 at about four A.M., weighing about 6 pounds, 12 ounces.

* * * * *

In the spring of 1888, Anna's horse, Caroline, gave birth to a male foal. She named him Chippewa.

ANDREW
NEW BREW MASTER

1891

Shortly after Joe and his younger sisters, Martha and Gretchen were born; life was becoming quite difficult for the young Fellerer family. Anna was struggling with having given birth to three babies in just three years and was quite alone with them all day while Andrew was at work at the brewery. Her struggle to keep up with the three new babies was compounded when the logging crews had moved away from their area, to cut logs further north, and this left Anna totally alone. She said to Andrew one evening after he returned from work, "I have seen several Indians in the area." "I know they are probably just hunting, and they may even be the Indians from that camp that you stayed at in that blizzard several years ago but they came right into our yard and I am scared."

Andrew responded, "I know that most of the Chippewa Indians around here are pretty harmless, but if you are worried, then I think it's time to sell our homestead and move in closer to the brewery." He was away at work for long days because of the distance from the brewery. Although he was doing quite well as the Maltster at the brewery, the malting process was a precise job. The temperature and timing had to be precise to create consistent batches of malt, and the kilning process was a slow process sometimes involving long hours to finish up a batch. He and Anna had been discussing the possibility of moving closer to the brewery for quite some time. They had even driven past the farmhouse just west of the brewery which had been vacant for some time. Anna said to Andrew, "That looks like a really nice house, it looks like it would make a very nice home for us, and it's so close to the brewery, you could walk to work."

Andrew replied, "Ok, I'll check on it and see if it's available." A short time later, Andrew caught up with his boss, Peter Schroeder, who was quite busy managing his other properties and business. He asked him, "You know that house just west of here, with a barn, and 40 acres? Do you know if it's available?"

Peter replied, "I'm glad you asked, yes I believe it is up for sale and I'm glad you are thinking of moving closer to the brewery because I'm considering promoting you to the Brew Master position. You have been doing such a great job as Maltster. And I have become too tied up with managing my other business to try and keep up with the Brew Master's job here. But you'll need to be available at all hours for the job, so you'll need to be close by."

Andrew replied excitedly, "I would most certainly accept the new job of Brew Master, I think I have enough knowledge of the brewing process to handle it."

"I believe you do," Peter said, "And, I believe you have the management skills, because you'll be running the whole brewery operation, because I'm really tied up right now with managing the new flour mill in Perham that I just bought, and also the saloon in Perham, and the one in the town of Frasier."

Then Andrew responded, "I'd like to start training in right away, and I'm going to head over to the saw mill and see if they can recommend a buyer for the Homestead."

"That's great," Peter stated, "then, I'll start finding someone to replace you as Maltster."

It was a bright sunny spring day and Andrew could hardly contain his excitement about the Brew Master promotion, "Anna will be so pleased to hear about it, and if I can get Clark & McClure to buy our homestead, everything will work out," he thought as he walked about a half block over to the saw mill. He walked into the office and asked to speak to Henry McClure. Henry's secretary said, "Henry is out on the waterfront, there's been a problem with the log chain that brings the logs up into the mill from the boom pond." Andrew walked down to the docks to find him. Here he looked out on the large boom pond which was filled with logs that had been floated down the river from White Pine Lake and even further upstream. The boom pond was formed by enhancing the falls to a height of about four feet by building a dam just above the falls. Several 'log jammers' were out on the logs directing them into the saw mill channel. He observed the long log chain just as they finished repairing it. A worker would direct a log down the narrow water channel with a long 'pike pole' and the teeth on the chain would grab the log and pull it up into the mill. Here it was rolled and clamped down onto the saw carriage, which ran past the saw on a set of rails. Then the mill operator would engage the carriage past the saw blade where the saw would slice off a slab of the log. The carriage was returned and the log rotated to remove another slab. When all four sides of the log were slabbed off, the operator would adjust the log position on the carriage to make cuts of boards to precise thickness as required. Some of the cuts were for 1 inch thick boards, and some were cut for 2 X 4's, and other 2 inch material for framing houses and other buildings. Some of the lumber was stacked outside to dry. Some was sold 'green', the demand was so great. Some lumber was loaded on railroad cars for shipment west to the town of Fargo and towns all across the Dakota Territory and eastern Montana.

Andrew then returned to the office area where Henry invited him into his office and said, "well, what brings you over here today, Andrew?"

"I'm here to talk about my homestead", Andrew replied directly. "I would like to know if you would be interested in purchasing my 180 acres, it has a very good stand of white pine on it. I was originally thinking of cutting the timber myself, but I have just been offered the Brew Master position at the brewery and have to move in closer".

"We would be very interested in purchasing the timber rights on it", Henry replied. "Here is how it works, I'll send a crew out to estimate the volume of timber, and we'll purchase it. I can tell you that there is a very good market right now for lumber. Then you'll have to list the property with a real estate agency to sell the actual piece of land. I can direct you to a good agency right near here that we use all the time."

Anna must have been overjoyed when Andrew came home from work that spring day in 1891, just a short time after Gretchen was born and announced to Anna, "I've been talking to my boss Peter, and he said that the house on the 40 acres next to the brewery is now for sale, and Peter also offered me the job of Brew Master as soon as we can get moved into that house." And, he said,"I've also talked to the people at the Clark and McClure sawmill, and they said they would be interested in buying the timber rights to our homestead."

"Oh, I am so proud of you Andrew," Anna exclaimed, "and I'm so thrilled and relieved," Anna went on to say, "now maybe I can get some help with the babies, Joseph, Martha and Gretchen. Now, you won't have to spend half your day on the road."

Andrew and Anna sold their homestead north of White Pine Lake later in 1891, after having lived there for about five years, because it was just too far from the brewery, about 12 miles. Which by horse and wagon, took Andrew about two hours each way to work and back every day, and he really needed to be closer to work because he was very excited about accepting Peter Schroeder's offer for the Brew Master position. Also, because it was located too far into Indian Territory.   He didn't want to leave his new wife and children, young Joe and Martha and baby Gretchen home alone during the day while he was at work at the brewery. They had heard about some troubles with the White Earth Chippewa Indians.

The Chippewa Indian people in Minnesota were a very peace-loving people. They were mostly eager to trade with the new settlers. In the early 1800's they traded regularly with the fur trappers. In the later 1800's they sold the pioneers and their lumber companies a lot of their timber which they had no use for at that time because they were a 'foraging and semi-nomadic' people, and just wanted to be left alone with their way of life. They were a very family and tribe oriented people. Most all of the stories of hostile Indians in this part of Minnesota were usually proved to be unfounded.

For the most part, the Chippewa people feared and respected the white settlers as long as the pioneers treated them fairly and allowed them to obtain the food they needed for survival. And mostly the pioneers respected the Indians. Proof of this relationship was that as time went on, more and more of the Chippewa and white settlers became married to each other, and settled all around the Perham area and raised families together.

In the late 1800's it was not uncommon to see Indians on the river in the fall, harvesting wild rice, or hunting game along the river banks. These were probably some of the Chippewa that had saved Andrew and Gretchen's life in that blizzard of 1887, or that Anna had encountered at the White Pine homestead before she and Andrew moved. The

White Earth Indian Reservation boundaries were not yet well established, and there was an encampment of the Chippewa just north of Big Pine Lake.

* * * * * *

When Andrew sold his homestead property, north of Big Pine Lake, he probably made a good profit on it. He bought it for probably a few cents an acre as homestead property, and after living on it for 5 years and improving it, he sold the timber rights to the Clark and McClure Lumber Company for a good price, and the land to a new settler. Late in the summer of 1891, after having sold their homestead, Andrew and Anna purchased the 40 acres of land with a house and barn on it just west of the brewery. As Anna began packing up their household, she commented to Andrew, "You know, we have added a lot of household things in the 5 years we've been here, with the new babies and everything. It's going to take a lot of trips back and forth to the new house to get all this stuff moved over there." So Andrew borrowed an extra wagon from one of their new neighbors near the brewery, and they hitched up Anna's horses, Caroline fend her foal, named Chippewa, now a 3 year old. As Andrew and Anna were moving their new family in, which at that time was their son Joe, age 3, and daughters Martha, age

2, and baby Gretchen. Anna remarked, "This new home will be so great for us Andrew, because you can now walk to work and I will have help with the babies, and I won't have to worry about the Indians." This house then, was the childhood home of Joe Fellerer and all of his brothers and sisters.

Just about 20 years before Andrew and Anna bought the 40 acres, this area was supposed to have been the new town site on the railroad line. In 1871, when the Northern Pacific Railroad first came across the Ottertail River, they had built a station house there. The new railroad passed in front of the Northern Pacific Steam Brewery, and between the brewery and the Clark and McClure Saw Mill. The railroad built their bridge over the dam and the falls. West of the saw mill was the highway bridge over the Ottertail River, for the road that ran southwest, and followed the Ottertail River to Rush Lake village, the very first settlement in the area. This railroad town site on the Ottertail River even had a Post Office and a general store and was to be called Naganoma. There were several houses and boarding houses built there for the saw mill and brewery workers. However, as the Northern Pacific Railroad pushed westward and onto the Prairie, the Railroad surveyed and laid out a new town site, and decided to move the town to the middle of the Prairie and named it 'Perham', after the president of the Northern Pacific Railroad. The station house and post office were then moved up onto the middle of the Perham prairie. Several other business and stores, were also moved from the town of Rush Lake, to the new town of Perham. Also from the town of Ottertail City, on the north shore of Ottertail Lake, several stores and business were relocated to the new town of Perham in the 1870's.

THE BREWERY

1891

In the 1800's running a large brewery operation was, as you can only imagine, quite a different world. The brewery was powered entirely by steam power. A steam boiler burned wood and a large steam engine powered the movement of the grains and malt thru out the building. It powered the grain elevators and the malt crushing mill. The water and beer were pumped by steam driven pumps. There was no electricity. Kerosene lamps were the only light source in the cellars and kegging room, and throughout the brewery at night.

The barley grain was hauled to the brewery Malting House by horse and wagon. In the 1800's most breweries did their own malting which involved spreading barley grain on the cement floor of the basement, and keeping it damp by spraying it frequently with water and turning it over frequently until a tiny sprout appeared about a sixteenth of an inch long. This then was malt. It was then sent to the Dry Kiln where it was dried and carefully roasted to just the right color for the type of beer that it would make. It was then crushed to release the sugars inside during the mashing phase. This malting process was the Maltster's job which Andrew started at when he started working at the brewery.

As Brew Master, Andrew's job was to manage the Brew House and the entire brewing process. The brew started with filling the mash tub with 162 degree water. Then the Malt was added bringing the mash temp, down to about 150 to 158 degrees. The malt to water ratio was about 1.5 qt., water to 1 lb. of malt. So for a 20 bbl. Brew, (the brew kettle was a 20 bbl. kettle) you would need about 350 gals. of water and 1070 lbs. of malt. Which was then, mixed in the mash tub. And the temp., held steady at 150 degrees for 1 hour, then brought up to 170 deg. Then it was sparged with about 250 gals. of 170 deg. water. This liquid from the mash is called 'wort', the name for unfermented beer. The wort was then tested with a hydrometer to make sure it had the right amount of converted sugars from the mash. A reading on the hydrometer scale of 1.042 would result in a finished beer of about 3 percent alcohol. It was then transferred to the brew kettle and hot water added to make a pre-boil volume of about 500 gals. starting brew, allowing for about 10 percent evaporation. The brewing, or boiling, lasted for about 1 hour. Hops were added at various times during the brew. These hops were imported from Germany.

To cool the wort down, after brewing in the brew kettle, ice was used, which was harvested from the river ice and stored in an insulated cellar called the Ice House. After cooling to about 50 deg., the wort was then transferred to the fermenting tank where yeast was added, and allowed to ferment for about 4 weeks, then moved to the lager tank.   The cellars where the beer was stored in large wooden tanks for aging, or 'lagering' did not require ice for cooling because the cellars were deep enough in the ground that the ambient temperature stayed at about 45 to 50 degrees year round, ideal to lager the beer. After 30 days in the lager the beer was kegged. The kegs of beer were hauled away by horse and wagon. Some of it was sold to local saloons in the area, such as Pete

Schroeder's saloons in Perham and Frazee, and some was loaded onboard the trains and shipped and sold all along the N.P. line as far west as Montana. The beer was selling very well, and was in very high demand. Andrew was an excellent Brew Master, and made a very good German lager. Peter Schroeder must have been very pleased with promoting him to the head position. Up until the bottling plant was built about 1906 the brewery only produced kegs of beer, these were wooden kegs of course. They were lined with pitch, which was made from pine tree sap. If a keg started to leak it was sprayed on the inside with this hot pitch, when it was returned to the brewery for a refill.

You may ask, why was the brewery such a prominent industry in Perham in the late 1800's? As this new land was being absorbed by more and more pioneers, these settlers were mostly 'middle European' and were mostly farmers. They brought with them the skills to quickly raise abundant crops of grain in the rich virgin soils of the prairies. Probably Wheat was their first crop of choice. In fact, there were numerous wheat mills, or flour mills scattered throughout the country. Probably every settlement had their own flour mill. Because the transporting of grain was a difficult process by horse and wagon, most grain crops had to be processed and consumed locally. Because of the skills of these early farmers, and the rich virgin soil, there was soon a surplus of these grains. These European immigrants also brought with them the necessary brewing skills to utilize the surplus crops of barley grain into making beer. Secondly, the beer itself up to that time was considered to be somewhat of a 'health' drink. This early beer, unlike today's beers, had a very low 'ABV' or alcoholic percentage, mostly around 1 to 3 percent. This was because of two reasons; first, the mashing process was not as efficient. This is where the starches and carbohydrates in the malt are converted into a simple sugar that can be fermented. Secondly, the yeast used back then had a much lower 'attenuation' or conversion efficiency of converting the sugars into alcohol. Therefore the resulting beer had a much higher ratio of starches, proteins, carbohydrates, and unfermented sugars remaining in the beer.

THE NEW AGE OF BEER

1905

In about 1900, the brewery was doing very well with Andrew as Brew Master. In the spring of 1900, Andrew called for a meeting to discuss expanding and upgrading the brewery. Andrew and Peter Schroeder got together in a meeting with their sales and brewery staff. Andrew opened the meeting by stating, "There are several issues that we need to discuss today. I've been noticing how out dated and worn out some of our equipment is becoming. There are several items that need to be replaced. Also, our sales are way up, the demand is so great that I'm now brewing sometimes three batches a day, and we still can't keep up, we need to expand our capacity."

The cellar manager added, "I'm doing all I can to keep up, but some of our tanks need to be replaced and our pumping equipment is just plan worn out and needs to be replaced."

Peter Schroeder commented, "Demand is up everywhere. New families are arriving every day. My flour mill can't keep up either. This is so great, we're making money, 'hand over fist', we can certainly afford to upgrade equipment and expand capacity."

"The other thing we need to discuss today," Andrew continued, "is this new trend that I've been hearing and reading about. People are demanding more and more bottled beer. I've heard that the bigger breweries south of us and in the Twin Cities have already installed bottling equipment, and in Duluth, Fitgers and Peoples breweries and going 'hole-hog' with bottled beer. We've got to keep up."

"I hear it all the time now from my sales people," the sales manager stated, "People in our area also want to be part of the new trend and are asking for bottled beer."

"Well, we can certainly afford to replace equipment and upgrade the brewery for bottled beer," Peter Schroeder stated, "The cash flow is excellent for all my businesses, especially the flour mill. How about the brewery, Andrew?"

"We can certainly afford to consider a major upgrade and expansion." Andrew replied, "And I like the idea of expanding into bottled beer. Peter and I will meet again to lay out the plans for this major project."

Andrew and Peter got together again later, to draw up plans for the expansion. They got together with an architect to design the building expansion. They also began shopping for new equipment. The capacity of the brewery was greatly increased and upgraded. A new 3 story brew house was built and a new 50 barrel brew kettle and mash tub was added along with many new and bigger lager tanks for the cellars, as well as a new steam boiler and steam engine.

Also built was a new bottling plant adjacent to the brew house. The bottling of beer was a very labor intensive process at the turn of the 19th century. The bottles were washed by hand, and filled on a filler machine one bottle at a time. The bottled beer was capped by a hand operated capper, which placed a wire 'harness' over the cap and around the neck of the bottle, similar to a champagne bottle. The bottles were then loaded into the pasteurizer. Here, the bottles were placed into a metal basket and lowered into a hot bath of 150 degree water for about 15 minutes, then moved to a tank of cooling water to return the beer bottles to room temperature. Labels were placed on the bottles by hand. These bottles were clear glass, and were the 'Belgian' style, 24 or 32 ounce size. Some half gallon sizes were also used. These early glass bottles, however were not very temperature change tolerant, and many broke during pasteurization.

DOWN THE DARK PATH

THE LONG ROAD TO

PROHIBITION

The United States has had a centuries long history of the widespread drinking of alcoholic beverages. It seems that right from the start, America was destined to become a culture of consumers of alcoholic beverages.

In 1630, the Puritans, among the first colonists from Europe, brought with them caches of beer and wine when they arrived on the East Coast. By the early 1700s, the American colonies already had a drinking problem. This was noted by Great Britain who instituted the first of many Prohibitions. In 1730, the British Parliament overseeing the American colonies, alarmed by the abuse of rum and brandy in the Georgia, colony, prohibited the transport of alcoholic beverages into the colony. But after the Georgians turned from farming to illegal stills and imported liquor from South Carolina, Parliament ended the prohibition after 13 years. (Ironically, the same number of years that Prohibition in the United States would last nearly two centuries later).

Commercial distillers of rum and whisky were well-established in the years before and after the Revolutionary War, as were many home brewers, including founding fathers George Washington and Thomas Jefferson. Taverns were the best places for social and political communications. They were the social media of the colonial times,

The second Continental Congress considered, but did not pass a bill to ban whiskey in 1777.

Dr. Benjamin Rush, Washington's surgeon general during the Revolutionary War, wrote in 1785 a pioneering and widely read argument for temperance, decrying the "ardent spirits" whiskey and rum as habit forming and associated with liver problems, diabetes, gout and madness. Rush however, did not object to people imbibing the lower-alcohol-content drinks, beer and wine.

President John Adams declared in 1811 his "zeal amounting to enthusiasm" against the spread of hard liquor and taverns.

Among the early organizations to protest excessive drinking was the Massachusetts Society for the Suppression of Intemperance, formed in 1814. Other groups in Connecticut and New York soon followed.

With better supplies of water available, President Andrew Jackson's Secretary of War eliminated the rations of whiskey given to soldiers in the U.S. Army and banned drinking at military installations.

The Washington Movement in Baltimore – a group of drinkers asking others to join in pledging to abstain from alcohol – started in 1840. Even a young Abraham Lincoln, in his "Temperance Speech" in 1842, praised the "splendid success" of campaigns to cut alcohol use, but asked crusaders to provide a "drop of honey" and "moral support" not condemnation for longtime drinkers.

The new "Temperance Movements" galvanized religious denominations, both Protestant and Catholic who viewed drinking as sinful. Maine became the first state to ban alcohol in 1851. This set off a national prohibition trend. Oregon, Rhode Island,

Massachusetts and Vermont went dry the next year and seven other states and one territory had prohibited alcohol by 1855. It didn't last long though, The Prohibitionists turned to a bigger issue -- abolishing slavery. When the Civil War broke out, the federal government needed the tax revenues on spirits and beer to finance the fight against the Southern rebellion. All of the prohibition states except Maine repealed their prohibition laws.

The Temperance Movement revived in the years after the Civil War, mostly among women who were the wives of middle and upper-class professional men.

After the Civil War, America was experiencing large waves of immigrants whose cultures included drinking alcoholic beverages; Ireland (Whisky) Germany (Beer) Italy and France (Wine).

By the early 19th century, heavy drinking became the norm among American men. The average adult male was consuming about 20 to 40 gallons of alcoholic beverages per year.

What was at first dubbed the "Women's War" against alcohol grew into a near-revolution and served as the country's first peaceful protest movement; a movement, that would influence the next generation. These women blamed domestic violence and financial problems in the home on drinking. They sought to disgrace men and close the many male-only saloons, or "dram shops," and breweries and distilleries through confrontations, picketing and "sit-in" protests.

THE PROHIBITIONISTS

1915

The Prohibition Party began as a small political party which promoted the banning of the manufacturing and sale of alcoholic beverages in the US. The party was formed in 1869. Another promoter of prohibition was the WCTU (Women's Christian Temperance Union), formed in 1872 headed by Francis Willard, who spoke of a national ban on alcohol. Their efforts would also promote women's suffrage. But their political successes were stunted because of lobbying by the moneyed liquor companies, which even blocked efforts to extend voting rights for women to prevent them from voting in favor of prohibition.

A larger shift in the path toward complete national Prohibition came in 1893 with the founding of the ASL(Anti-Saloon League), a prohibitionist group that involved fewer women and was headed by a man, Wayne Wheeler, who proved to be a shrewd, ruthless political tactician. The league debuted during a period known as the Progressive Era that produced reforms in civil rights, labor, conservation and industry. Wheeler capitalized on the anti-immigrant sentiment of the age, inducing fear among mainly rural white Americans that the drinking cultures of new arrivals from Europe in urban areas were weakening the nation's moral fiber. He first succeeded in getting "dry" legislators elected in Ohio. By 1908, more than 50 counties in Ohio opted to ban alcohol. Wheeler and his ASL realized that national prohibition was within their grasp.

WAYNE WHEELER, (DRY BOSS)
(from Wikipedia)

Wayne Bidwell Wheeler (November10, 1869 to September 5, 1927, was an American attorney and Prohibitionist. His most famous contribution to the prohibition movement was when he joined the Anti-Saloon League and greatly influenced the creation of the Eighteenth Amendment and the National Prohibition Act (The Volstead Act).

Wheeler was born in Brookfield Township, Ohio. His anti-alcohol stance started as a young lad working on his family's farm, when he came across an intoxicated hired hand who was so drunk that he was unaware of what he was doing with his pitchfork until it had been accidentally lodged into the leg of the young Wheeler. He also observed another drunken worker threaten and frighten his mother and sisters. These events appear to have traumatized him and led to his antipathy to drinking.

After graduating with a B.A. from Oberlin College in 1894, Wheeler accepted employment as an organizer for the recently established Anti-Saloon League. While continuing to work full time with the ASL, he attended Western Reserve Law School. He graduated in 1898 and promptly became attorney for the ASL, an organization to which he devoted the rest of his life.

Early in his career, Wheeler showed strong organizational skills and political acumen. In 1915, he moved to Washington, DC, where he could more easily wield important political pressure. He soon developed what is now known as pressure politics, or "Wheelerism".

Under Wheeler's leadership, the League focused on the goal of achieving National Prohibition. Unlike Francis Willard's Women's Christian Temperance Union, which dealt with many humanitarian issues, Wheeler felt that the only way to successfully challenge the political influence of the Brewers Lobby, was to focus purely on achieving national prohibition by any means necessary. Wheeler was able to get "dry" politicians elected by encouraging the "drys" of both political parties to vote for a single candidate who supported the "dry" cause, regardless of the party the candidate was affiliated with, completely disregarding party affiliation on other issues. Unlike other temperance groups, the ASL worked with the two major parties rather than backing the smaller Prohibition Party.

Wheeler frequently claimed to have essentially written the National Prohibition Enforcement Act (The Volstead Act.) Congressman Volstead repeatedly denied that assertion. However, it is clear that Wheeler was at least highly influential in drafting its contents.

By 1926, after Prohibition had begun, The Prohibition Bureau began adding poisons to industrial alcohol to prevent its use as a beverage. Wheeler opposed the use of nonpoisonous denaturants such as soap or other noxious but harmless chemicals. He argued that "the government us under no obligation to furnish people with alcohol that is drinkable in any way when the Eighteenth Amendment prohibits it. The person who drinks this industrial alcohol is a deliberate suicide." These sorts of views and the severity of his opinions began to change the way the public viewed the Anti-Saloon

League after bad alcohol killed at least 50,000 people during the course of Prohibition

Wheeler retired shortly after; on Andrew 14, 1927 and returned to Little Point Sable, Ohio. Wheeler died just two weeks after losing his wife and father-in-law in a burn accident. He died at the age of 57.

Prohibition was considered a dismal failure that created more problems than it solved. Only one in five adults in the country supported making drinking illegal. Many more supported "neo-prohibition."

Wayne Wheeler is not widely heard of today; however, many who are familiar with Prohibition regard him as playing one of the most important roles in the creation of the 18th Amendment. His use of pressure politics, his expertise in rallying the "dry" base, and the sheer amount of time and effort he contributed to the ASL, were the key staples in the success of the ASL, and the Prohibition movement as a whole. Without Wayne B. Wheeler's generalship, it is more than likely we would never have had the Eighteenth Amendment.

THE WOMENS CHRISTIAN TEMPERANCE UNION

The WCTU was a very vocal and militant group. They began staging demonstrations and rallies all across the country. Gradually they influenced several state governments to enact prohibition legislation, forbidding the sale and manufacturing of alcoholic beverages. These states became known as, "Dry States".

Through the efforts of these Prohibitionists, by 1915, about 50% of the American people already lived under total Prohibition.

The first two decades of the 20th century were becoming very prosperous times for the entire country. More and more new consumer products were being invented and marketed. New factories were being built, offering more jobs. An example was the new and burgeoning automobile industry.

Electricity was becoming available to more cities all across America. But there was a very dark side to all this prosperity. While the American workers were making more disposable income, they were also partying and drinking more.

In the late 1800's and early 1900's, the per-capita consumption of alcoholic beverages peaked at a staggering 20, to as much as 40 gallons of booze per person, per year. It shouldn't be too surprising, to see these 'anti-drinking' organizations, such as the Prohibition Party and the WCTU were getting a foothold in the political arena. These groups became very active in Minnesota by 1915. They staged demonstrations in many of the cities and towns in the state. especially, those which harbored a brewery.

* * * * * *

In about 1915, these 'Prohibitionists' staged a demonstration and rally at the Schroeder Perham brewery. On the day of the rally, they blocked entry and exit from the brewery and stopped all beer wagons from leaving with loads of beer, and by late afternoon the crowd captured and overturned a wagon load of beer cases, breaking and smashing the entire load of beer. Then later that evening, they broke into the brewery building and set fire to the malting section. Andrew and his crew were able to extinguish the fire, but extensive damage was done to the upper floor of the malt storage area.

The dark clouds of Prohibition were looming across America.

In 1915, the Prohibition Party, along with the WCTU and the Anti Saloon League exerted enough pressure, politically, in Minnesota, to cause the Minnesota Commission of Public Safety to issue an order that closed all the breweries and saloons in the area of the state that was outlined as 'Indian reservation land' in the Indian treaty of 1855. This treaty, forbid the sale and manufacture of alcoholic beverages on or near Indian lands. This action dealt a harsh blow to Peter Schroeder and the brewery at Perham. They forced him to close his brewery and also his saloons in Perham and Frasier, along with other financial problems with some of Peter Schroeder's other business, such as the Globe Mill in Perham. This caused him to place ownership of the brewery with the Perham Holding Company. By

1917, however, after much political haggling, the breweries and saloons were again allowed to open and the Perham Brewery reopened.

Like a huge black thunder storm cloud, rolling across the prairie, in early 1917,

The dark clouds of War were descending upon the whole world, and at the same time, the dark clouds of Prohibition were descending upon The United States of America.

PROHIBITION

THE NOBLE EXPERIMENT

How did this happen?

It was President Hoover who coined the phrase: ***"The Noble Experiment"***.

The Eighteenth Amendment to the U.S. Constitution went into effect on January 16, 1920.

It wiped out the beer, the breweries, the distilleries; the wineries and the culture that had come to define American social life. We look back on the Noble Experiment called Prohibition today and we can't even understand how this could happen. What were people thinking back then?

Well, ironically, things weren't too different back then, than they are today in a number of ways. Economic turmoil, corporate greed, a widening gap between the rich and poor, immigration issues, scandal-filled tabloid headlines, a middle class worried about the direction of the country. It sounds like today's TV news headlines. But these were the same problems facing American society at the turn of the 20th century.

Over the last decades of the 1800s, rapid industrialization and unprecedented immigration in America created a country of big cities and booming growth. A lot of reforms were implemented in the early years of the twentieth century; the forty-hour work week, labor unions, child labor laws, minimum wages. But the very prosperous times with American workers having more disposable income led to the development of a "saloon-culture".

Sometimes with all of the technology that we have in today's world, it's hard for us to imagine life without it. Those pre-prohibition times were before the advent of the great inventions of our times. Before the invention of the automobile, the radio or television, cell phones, computers, or the internet.

Practically the only social outlet for the working class, were the saloons. They were the "social-media" of those times. The saloons provided a platform for the open discussions of social and political issues of the times. And they were everywhere, often four or five on the same block in the cities and towns of America. But the dark side of the saloon atmosphere was that it also provided for a culture of drinking.

Powerful Women
And
Power Politics

In January 1917, the 65th Congress convened, in which the "dries" outnumbered the "wets" by 140 to 64 in the Democratic Party and 138 to 62 among Republicans, thanks largely to the efforts of the WCTU and ASL, (Anti-saloon League).

Many city residents in America resented the scores of saloons in their communities that enticed working men to squander their money on booze and other vices. But for the national prohibitionists, the major tipping point in their "dry" campaign was World War 1. After America declared war on Germany in April 1917, Wheeler and his alliance of women's temperance bands such as the ASL, the Prohibition Party, the WCTU and other protestant

Church groups set their sights on a constitutional amendment banning the creation of most alcoholic beverages in the United States.

Wheeler and his army of Prohibitionists made for a powerful national political force. They exploited patriotism and created resentment against German American beer makers, and to protect U.S. troops from the temptations of liquor and saloons. With America's declaration of war against Germany, German Americans – a major force against prohibition, and many of the prominent brewers of the day were widely discredited and their protests subsequently ignored.

Wheeler's first big triumph was convincing Congress to approve a Wartime Prohibition, a ban on the manufacture of alcohol for the duration of the war, to preserve the grain crops for the war effort. The War Prohibition Act went into effect on July 1, 1917.

With the momentum on their side, these "dry" activists proposed a Prohibition Amendment to Congress and lobbied state legislatures to approve its passage. Wheeler was instrumental in drafting the new amendment.

ANDREW VOLSTEAD

THE 18th AMENDMENT TO
THE US CONSTITUTION

THE VOLSTEAD ACT

It was a cold and blustery December day in Washington, D.C. in 1917. A young Senator from Minnesota made his way from his office in the Senate Office Building to the Capitol. In his briefcase he carried his final draft of a new bill. There were twelve hundred pages of it. The bill had already passed Committee, and he would submit it to the House for a vote. When it passed there, it would be forwarded to the full Senate for a majority vote.

The bill would have his name on it. He was Andrew Volstead, Senator from Minnesota's 10th Congressional district in the town of Granite Falls. This bill, when passed, would forbid the manufacture, distribution, and sale of all alcoholic beverages in the United States.

The bill passed both the House and the Senate by December 18, 1917. It was then sent to President Woodrow Wilson for signing, however, the signing was postponed because of World War One. President Wilson instead issued an executive order prohibiting the sale of grain for the manufacture of alcoholic beverages because of the war. However, most manufactures of alcoholic beverages had already stockpiled enough grain to get them through the war.

As American soldiers were dying on the battlefields of Europe, the U.S. Senate, on August 1st, 1917 passed a resolution containing the language of the 18th Amendment, which was to be presented to the states for ratification.

* * * * *

In 1919 The President signed the bill, which became known as the Volstead Act. It then had to be ratified by three fourths of the states. After the ratification by 36 states, the bill became the 18th amendment to the constitution.

On January 16th, 1920 Prohibition began- - - - .

TEXT OF THE 18ᵗʰ AMENDMENT

Section 1. *After one year from the ratification of this article, the manufacture, sale, or transportation of intoxicating liquors within, the importation thereof into, or the exportation thereof from the United States and all the territory subject to the jurisdiction thereof for beverage purposes is hereby prohibited.*

Section 2. *The Congress and the several States shall have concurrent power to enforce this article by appropriate legislation.*

Section 3. *This article shall be inoperative unless it shall have been ratified as an amendment to the Constitution by the legislatures of the several States, as provided in the Constitution, within seven years from the date of the submission hereof to the States by the Congress.*

The vote was 65 to 20, with the Democrats voting 36 in favor and 12 in opposition; and the Republicans voting 29 in favor and 8 in opposition.

The House of Representatives passed a revised resolution on December 17, 1917 In the House, the vote was 282 to 128, with the Democrats voting 141 in favor and 64 in opposition; and the Republicans voting 137 in favor and 62 in opposition. Four Independents in the House voted in favor and two Independents cast votes against the amendment.

It was officially proposed by the Congress to the states when the Senate passed the resolution by a vote of 47 to 8, the next day, December18th, 1917

The amendment and its enabling legislation did not ban the consumption of alcohol, but made it impossible to obtain alcoholic beverages legally, as it prohibited the manufacture, sale and distribution of them anywhere in the United Sates and the U.S. territories.

THE WAR TO END ALL WAR

WORLD WAR 1

In April, 1917 the US declared war on Germany and on July 11, 1918 Joe Fellerer, the son of Andrew Fellerer, Brew Master of the Schroeder Brewery at Perham received a notice from the local draft board to report for military duty on July 22, 1918.

He was sent to Fort Greene, North Carolina for basic training and assigned to the 3rd Pioneer Infantry Division. At Fort Greene, Joe was assigned to a supply Company in the Division and was issued a team of mules and a wagon

After about 2 months of training the 3rd Pioneer Infantry Division was called up to be shipped overseas for duty in France.

THE HOME FRONT

Back home on the farm, Joe's absence after being pulled off the farm for war duty was being sorely felt. Everyone had to step up to fill in for the work that Joe had done. Joe's dad had to find extra time off from the brewery and pitch in with field work. And Joe's sisters also had to do more of the farm chores.

Anna Fellerer, Joe's mother, was also impacted with an additional burden. Because this was a war with Germany, most of the German immigrant families had close relatives in Germany, and some of the immigrants were outspoken opponents of the war. The War Department along with the Department of Immigration and the Department of Justice required that all immigrants from Germany who were not yet citizens had to be accounted for and registered as being from Germany. Anna was not yet a US citizen so she was issued an ID which she was required to carry at all times that stated that she was an immigrant from Germany. This caused a lot of stress for Anna and Andrew and probably the whole family. Not so much the alien registration card, but the fact that they had a lot of close relatives in Germany whom they communicated with regularly. Now it became a lot more difficult to get mail into and out of Germany. Probably a bigger worry for Anna and Andrew was that Joe could actually be fighting against some of his cousins in Germany. But the biggest worry for them was for Joe's safety as they knew he was about to be put in harm's way.

PERIL AT SEA

After being called up for duty on the war front in France, the Division and all their equipment were loaded aboard a ship for transport to France. The ship was a 'side-wheeler', that is, it had a huge paddle wheel on the side of the ship in the middle.

The trip across the Atlantic was not without its perils and dangers. Joe's first few days were trying, as he and most of the other soldiers struggled to overcome seasickness. And worse, Joe and several of his unit had their bunks right next to the huge paddle wheel which rumbled like thunder day and night from the wheel, but mostly from the huge drive arm that powered the wheel, very much like a steam locomotive had, because like a locomotive, the ship was powered by coal and steam.

The soldiers had duties to perform on board, there was the usual kitchen duty and clean-up. The soldiers that had horses or mules assigned to them had to keep them fed and watered, and cleaned up after. The manure was then dumped overboard. There was also watch duty on deck. There was 24 hour watch and each soldier had a rotation of six hours. Because at that time there was no radar or sonar they depended on physical sightings of possible German U-boats or destroyers. There were five soldiers on the fore deck and 4fouron the stern deck. Joe actually welcomed his watch duty because it got him up on deck away from the noise of the paddle wheel and heat of the boilers.

About six days at sea they ran into a terrible storm, probably a tropical storm or hurricane. It was that time of the year. There was no tracking or prediction of these storms back then, (no satellite radar). Joe said the storm lasted about three days. One day while he was on watch duty on the fore deck, back near the bulkhead. He saw waves wash over the bow. The ship was loaded so heavily that it rode low in the water. One of the waves was so large and powerful that it swept away the forward watchman. Joe said that he watched the soldier standing there at the rail and the wave came up over the rail, and the guy was just gone, disappeared into the sea. Any type of rescue was impossible in that storm. After the storm they had a memorial service for him, and his family was later notified. He was the first casualty for the 3rd Pioneer Infantry Division. After that the watchmen were required to be tethered to the railing or bulkhead during any rough weather.

Then water was coming into the lower decks from the high seas and they had to man the pumps to keep the lower decks from flooding. The ship had a few pumps that were steam driven, but many more that were man powered. It required two men to a pump for hours then changing hands. The storm was doing other damage to the ship as well. The high seas and the low riding ship resulted in the paddle wheel completely submerging, causing too much strain on the drive arm and the shaft and paddles. Something ended up being bent, but they couldn't fix it at sea. So the ship limped along at about half speed and made a horrible noise. Finally in about four weeks they reached port in France. Joe said that later he heard that the ship was scuttled and not repaired as it was very old and outdated. He said when he came home after the war he had a newer screw drive ship,

much faster and to Joe's delight, quieter. Joe said
that he never told his Ma and Pa about the storm at
sea. He didn't want to worry them.

GET THE KAISER

The term, 'Kaiser', in German, meant Emperor, and referred to Kaiser Wilhelm II, the Emperor of Germany. And the phrase 'Get the Kaiser', was the 'battle cry' of World War 1.

Upon arrival in France, the 3rd Pioneer Infantry Div. was dispatched to the front. Joe's job was to haul supplies up to the front lines, to the trenches, from a supply depot at the rear. The supplies include ammunition, food, clothing and other supplies. Joe performed his duties, along with the other drivers, driving his mule team and wagon and avoiding the constant barrage of exploding artillery shells. Between the supply runs, he busied himself writing many letters home.

* * * * * *

Joe told this story about one of his first such trips up to the front lines. Just as he approached the trenches where the 3rd Pioneer Infantry was encamped, there was a terrible barrage of artillery shells exploding all around him and his mule team and wagon. The mules become so spooked by the shelling that Joe lost control of them and they just took off running, and they ended up in one of the trenches. The wagon was tipped on its side. The soldiers nearby yelled at him, to cover the mules heads, to calm them. So Joe covered their heads with a blanket. This calmed them down, but the barrage continued and Joe took cover in a tunneled bunker with the other soldiers. But the barrage continued on into the night, so Joe had to spend the night in the bunker. By morning the shelling had stopped so they unloaded the wagon and got it tipped upright. They then all pushed and helped him get up out of the trench. After that, Joe carried a blanket with him on his supply runs and if there was more shelling he stopped and covered the mules heads and this calmed them down. Toward the end of the war he was issued a truck for his deliveries.

The war ground on and the front lines moved back and forth from trench to trench. As the war was nearing the end, the fighting intensified and the casualties increased. The rumors spread, as they always do in armies, that there were peace talks going on in Versailles. Meantime Joe was sometimes ordered to load wounded soldiers in his truck on the return trips from his supply runs to be dropped off at the hospital. These were supposed to be lightly wounded. The seriously wounded went by ambulances. On one such trip he picked up three wounded who were loaded on stretchers into the back of his truck, but by the time he got them back to the hospital, all three were dead. Apparently those three should have been on an ambulance, because he had no medic with him. He then delivered them to the morgue.

THE END OF THE WAR

TO END WARS

1919

On what would be his final run to the front lines he was ordered to report to the rear command tent. There he was given a courier packet to be delivered to his divisional commander at the front lines. He then reported to the divisional command tent with the packet. He was told to wait and carry the reply back to rear command just as he'd done before. The message was de-coded and the divisional commander read it to his staff. The message said; "PULL BACK – PULL BACK – VERSAILLES HAS SIGNED – THE WAR IS OVER!" The division commander looked at Joe and said, 'there is no reply Corporal Fellerer, we're going home'.

So the war that was 'to end all wars' ended with the signing of the peace treaty at Versailles and Germany surrendering on November 11, 1918.

Joe and the 3rd Pioneer Division traveled to Paris for the giant victory parade down the Champs Elysses and under the Arc De Triomphe. Joe and some other soldiers traveled to Monte Carlo on the southern coast of France while they waited for a ship to take them home. Soon ships became available and Joe and the rest of the division were put on a ship to return home. He arrived home late in the year of 1919.

EIGHTEENTH AMENDMENT TO THE

UNITED STATES CONSTITUTION

(Amendment XVIII) of the United States Constitution effectively established the prohibition of alcoholic beverages in the United States of America and its territories by declaring the production, transport, and sale of alcohol (though not the consumption or private possession) illegal. The separate National Prohibition Act (Volstead Act) set down methods for enforcing the Eighteenth Amendment, and defined which "intoxicating liquors" were prohibited, and which were excluded from prohibition (e.g. for medical and religious purposes and industrial uses).

The Eighteenth Amendment was the first amendment to set a time delay before it would take effect following ratification, and the first to set a time limit for its ratification by the states. Many state legislatures had already enacted statewide prohibitions prior to the ratification of the Eighteenth Amendment, By 1916, 23 of the 48 states had already passed laws against saloons, some even banning the manufacture of alcoholic beverages in their states.

When the House and the Senate both passed the resolution for the 18th Amendment, it was officially proposed by the Congress to be turned over to the states for ratification; on December 18th 1917. The Amendment required ratification by 36 of the 48 states.

The state of Mississippi was the first state to ratify the Amendment, on January 7, 1918. The ratification of the Amendment was completed on January 16, 1919; when Nebraska became the 36th state of the 48 then in the Union to ratify it. However, interesting enough, Minnesota was number 39 but didn't complete its ratification until January 17, 1919. Wisconsin, did it the same day at number 40

Prohibition began on January 16. 1920.

ANDREW VOLSTEAD
(from Wikipedia)

Andrew John Volstead (October 31, 1860 to January 20, 1947) was a Republican member of the United States House of Representatives from 1903 to 1923. His name is closely associated with the National Prohibition Act of 1919, which informally carries his name, "The Volstead Act." The act was the enabling legislation for the enforcement of Prohibition in the United States beginning in 1920.

Volstead was born in the town of Kenyon, Goodhue County, Minnesota; to Norwegian-American parents. He was educated at St. Olaf College in Minnesota, where he received his law degree and served as mayor of Granite Falls, Minnesota, from 1900 to 1902.

While in Congress, he served as chairman of the House Judiciary Committee from 1919 to 1923. Although often considered the author of the Volstead

Act, he collaborated with Wayne Wheeler of the Anti-Saloon League, who conceived and largely drafted the bill. However, Volstead sponsored the bill and championed, promoted and facilitated its passage.

Volstead was a member of the 58th through the 67th congresses. He was defeated in his attempt to be elected to an 11th term in 1922. Shortly thereafter he was hired as legal adviser to the chief of the National Prohibition Enforcement Bureau.

Upon Repeal of Prohibition in 1933, Volstead returned to Granite Falls, Minnesota, where he resumed his private law practice. He died in 1947. Volstead's former home, located at 163 Ninth Avenue, Granite Falls, Minnesota is a National Historic Landmark.

NATIONAL PROHIBITION ACT
(VOLSTEAD ACT)

Writers of the Eighteenth Amendment to the Constitution took a little more than one hundred words to prohibit the manufacture, sale and transportation of alcoholic beverages in the U.S. It fell to Minnesota Congressman Andrew Volstead, Chairman of the House Judiciary Committee to write the regulations and rules for its enforcement.

The twelve thousand word Volstead Act remained in effect for thirteen years, from 1920 until Prohibition was repealed in December 1933.

The Eighteenth Amendment required one year between ratification by the states and the beginning of enforcement. Congress needed that time to create the new law's specific regulations. Minnesota Congressman Andrew Volstead, as chairman of the House Judiciary Committee, was responsible for writing the National Prohibition Act. The stern-faced congressman from Granite Falls set out to moderate the strict philosophy of the amendment's primary promoting group, The Anti-Saloon League. They and other unwavering prohibitionists had sought to prevent even one drop of alcohol from being produced and sold.

Volstead struck a balanced approach between the spirit of the law and practical realities. His legislation continued the producing of existing prescriptions of alcohol for medical purposes, and denatured alcohol for industrial uses. It also allowed for the brewing and sale of what was called "near-beer" with an alcoholic content of no more than one half of one percent, and the home manufacturing of alcoholic, but "non-intoxicating," fruit juice and cider. Volstead said that he put in as much alcohol as the Congress would stand for.

Yet the amendment was not without its controversies. The phrase "intoxicating liquor" would not logically, nor legally have included beer and wine. These drinks were much lower alcohol than whiskey and other "hard" liquors, and their inclusion in the Prohibition Amendment came as a surprise o the general public, as well as beer and wine makers.

Prohibition as enforced by the Volstead Act transformed American streets, businesses, and the social life of America for an entire generation and beyond. The streetscapes of American cities were forever changed. In the little town of Little Falls, Minnesota, the town's fourteen saloons closed overnight, with some of the owners now selling soft drinks and ice-cream sundaes. Some began selling the non-alcoholic malt beverages. The new "buzz-word" of the day was "near-beer"

Some would never again be open for business. In the Twin Cities, the Salvation Army turned some beer parlors into canteens for the entertainment of returning soldiers and sailors from World War I, serving sodas and ice cream.

Enterprising businessmen quickly recognized opportunities in non-alcoholic beverages. Many former saloon owners quickly replaced their liquor bar with a soda fountain and ice cream bar for their pool halls. To take advantage of increasing sales of soft drinks, companies including the Minneapolis based Brazilla soft drink company created new fruit and cola flavors. Popular treats described in soda fountain trade journals included the Prohibition Sour, the Flapper Frappe, and the Dry Days Sundae.

THE BOOTLEGGERS

(Webster's dictionary defines "bootlegging" as hiding illegal booze in one's boot leg.)

The term was coined during the prohibition years; when apparently the fashion for men was a high-top boot, as high as the knee and loosely fashioned at the top; generally to accommodate tucking ones pant-leg into the boot. These boot tops would then be used by the buyer or seller of illegal booze to hide one, or several bottles of the illegal booze in the boot top while escaping the law.

Not everyone in the general public supported the Eighteenth Amendment and the Volstead Act's restrictions. Volstead's mail reflected both approval and disapproval of the law that took his name.

Minnesota newspapers reported on local raids and the arrests of the traveling Bootleggers. One raid at the Preiss brewery in St. Cloud, Minnesota resulted in five arrests for brewing beer of more than 2.5 percent alcohol which was much higher than the Volstead Act's limitation of ".05" per cent alcohol. At the Remmler plant in Red Wing, Minnesota beer as high as 3 percent was found. Those tempted to make or consume home brewed moonshine were regularly confronted with front-page stories about people who had died from drinking bad booze with the empty bottles by their side.

Newspaper editorials in the Bemidji, Minnesota paper urged their readers to follow the Volstead Act laws. "People who bought illegal alcoholic beverages or went to speakeasies," they warned, "were as guilty as the bootleggers or moonshiners in promoting a destructive atmosphere of lawlessness."

* * * * *

THE ROARING TWENTIES

THE BOOTLEGGING YEARS

It was the early 1920's. The Prohibition years were just beginning.

On a warm spring evening in 1922, just after dark, Andrew and his son Joe pulled the team of horses and wagon down into the woods behind the granary of their farm. There they unloaded the load of equipment from the now shuttered brewery. This was the first load that they bought from Peter Schroeder and the Otter Falls Holding Company, which now owned all of the brewery equipment when prohibition shut it down. This first load contained a 100 gallon copper pot that had been the rice and corn cooker in the old Schroeder brewery, and now would become the brew kettle. Also on the load were two of the smaller 100 gallon wooden fermenting tanks from the brewery.

Carefully they maneuvered these pieces into position into the still open end of the basement of the 'hog-kitchen' which they were building between the granary and the hog barn. When these were properly positioned, they returned to the old shuttered brewery for another load of the equipment that they bought from Peter and the holding company. This load contained a 300 gallon steel water tank. Another load contained two of the 200 gallon wooden lager tanks. These also they positioned into the basement. The last load contained a wort filter and cooler and the beer kegging equipment and about twenty of the 'half-barrel beer kegs, along with a bottle filler and about fifty cases of beer bottles.

In the next few days, they would pour a cement floor over the basement and seal up the back wall. In the back wall, they put a door. The equipment and the basement would be concealed from detection from above, or anywhere else around the building. Access to this basement brew chamber would be through a secret 'steel-clad' door in the well room, which was in the granary basement. The well was covered with thick oak planks and a trap door.

Another steel clad door, in the back, would open into a tunnel that would run down the hillside to the edge of the tamarack swamp. This was all covered over by dirt to conceal it. When the cement floor was dry, they would complete the ground floor of the building with brick walls, windows and doors, a roof, and a large, tall brick chimney. Inside the main floor they would install a wood burning boiler for steam heat, and the large three hundred gallon water tank above a fire box. These would also be used to heat the hog swill, which has many of the same ingredients as a beer mash.

* * * * * *

Frank came down from the 'hog kitchen' above into the granary basement and entered the brew house through the steel door. "The water in the hot water tank is at 170 degrees," he announced, "you can go ahead with the sparge."

"Ok," Joe replied, "The mash is at a reading of 1.065 gravity. I'll open the valve to start the sparge. It looks like we got the corn adjunct ratio right this time at one third volume of the mash. That bumps up our original gravity, nicely to the 1.065 range."

"So," Frank said, "That means the ABV of the batch will be around eight or nine percent. Boy, that's a lot higher than we used to brew in the old brewery before prohibition."

"Yah, that's right, Henry added from over in the corner office where he sat behind the desk doing the bookkeeping, "but it's what all the speak-easy's want these days. They say that people coming in for drinks want their alcohol and are willing to pay for it. I guess they feel they are taking the risk going there, so they want a high powered drink. Our net profit this year for the higher ABV beer is up about eighty per cent."

"Wow," Joe said, "you mean they're paying a dollar a glass for our beer, and our take is a half dollar. That's way more profitable than farming."

"Yah," Henry said, "Lewis is doing a great job selling."

"So, how much money are we making?" Frank asked.

"You know I can't tell you that, Frank," Henry replied, "because even I don't know what our quarterly totals are. Pa does those himself, and also does the banking. He has us all sworn to secrecy about all of the functions of the operation. Aside from Lewis, we don't know who the sellers or the delivery people are. He's set it up that way so that if anyone of us is arrested by the ATF officers, we can't give them anyone else's information."

"Speaking of the 'revenuers'," Joe said. "You may have noticed them coming down to the old brewery about once a month, just poking around the place to make sure nothing is being produced there anymore. I think they know that there is some beer being produced somewhere in central Minnesota, they just don't know where. I've read in the Otter Falls paper about several speak-easies being raided over by Brainerd recently."

"They came to the farm just last week," Frank said, "Joe and I were just busy feeding the hogs. It looks like our operation is pretty fool proof. There's no way for anyone to know if we are preparing a batch of hog swill in the mixing tank upstairs, or mixing a tank full of mash."

After a ten minute sparging of the mash in the tank above, Joe opened the valve and drained the wert from the mash into the brew kettle. Next, he opened the steam valve to allow the hot steam lines inside the kettle to bring the wert up to boiling temperature. The brewing phase would last one hour, with hops added at the beginning and at the last ten minutes of the brew.

As the brew was starting to boil, Joe said, "Ok, boys, let's start kegging and bottling that vat of lager that's finished and ready to be sold."

Henry went to work on the kegging machine and Joe and Frank set to work on the bottling machine. Just as they were finishing the batch, Andrew came in through the tunnel. The tunnel went out through the back wall of the basement, which was secured by another steel door, and went down the steep hillside and came out at the edge of the tamarack swamp, where a narrow water canal had been created along the edge of the swamp, obscured from view by brush and cattails and connected to the river. Canoes would come up the canal in the middle of the night, from the river, and load the bootlegged beer, to be taken down stream for distribution in towns all along the Ottertail River, where there were speak-easies. It was sold all the way to Breckenridge on the Red River, and north to Moorhead and Fargo. In winter the bootleg beer was loaded onto the farm truck and covered with a load of hay, or a load of grain.

As Andrew came in from the tunnel, Joe said to him, "We've got another batch ready to go and a new batch in the brew kettle."

"Good," Andrew said, "Let's get this batch down to the canal for pickup tonight. When we get that done, I've got an announcement to make."

So, Joe, Andrew, Frank and Peter began carrying the kegs and cases of the bootleg beer out the tunnel and down to the pickup spot on the canal. The shippers would be arriving soon, in their canoes at about twenty minute intervals, to haul away the bootleg stash. When they completed carrying the batch down the tunnel, they all came back in and Andrew locked the tunnel door and turned to them.

"I've got some very bad news, boys. This may just put an end to our entire operation. I've just learned that Lewis has been arrested for selling our bootleg beer, along with his head salesman, Fred Buchanen and the owner of 'The Wild River Club', in Moorhead, one of our biggest client speak-easies. Apparently the ATF raided the speak-easy while Lewis and Fred were there delivering a shipment of our beer. I've been told that they initially escaped, but were chased all the way to Thief River Falls, where they were stopped by the local police for speeding as they came into town. The ATF officers caught up with them and arrested them. The good news, if you could call it that, is that the ATF is thinking they were selling the booze from a still and bootleg brewery in Thief River Falls. So, at least for now, we haven't been implicated."

"Looks like Lewis is going to need an attorney," Joe stated.

"Yah, I'll go up to Thief River Falls tomorrow and get one on retainer. His hearing is day after tomorrow."

"Should we go with," Frank questioned?"

"Nah, we all need to stay far away from any of those ATF boys," Andrew stated.

So, for now, let's get the equipment scrubbed down and run that last batch out of the brew kettle and through the cooler into the fermenter. That may just be our last batch, depending on what happens to Lewis."

The Fellerer brothers finished the cleanup, and Andrew moved the last batch into the fermenter and Joe added the yeast and cleaned the brew kettle and cooler. When finished, they all left the secret brewery chamber.

THE END OF BOOTLEGGING

This time it was Andrew, coming in through the steel door, carrying a large satchel. He lit the lamps and went over to the desk in the office corner and got a key out of a drawer and went over to the safe and unlocked it. From it he took twelve bundles of paper money and a stack of other papers, along with the key to the steel door. He put all this into his large satchel. He reached into the safe again and pulled out two solid gold bars. He carried them over to the tunnel entrance, unlocked the door and disappeared down the tunnel. A few minutes later, he reappeared and walked over to the safe and extracted another set of the gold ingots and again disappeared into the tunnel with them. He made two more trips from safe to tunnel and returned and took out the leather folio and wrote something on the back of one of the sheets and put it back into the folio and returned the folio to the safe and locked it and put the key back in the desk drawer. Shortly after that, several large explosions were heard, and a cloud of dust rolled out of the tunnel entrance, followed by Joe, Frank and Peter. They came in covered in dust and carrying several sacks of cement.

"Well, we blew up the tunnel," Joe announced, "all the way from just past the chimney base, down to the swamp."

"Ok, that's good, boys," Andrew said, "Now while I make a run with the last of our cash, you three can mix up the cement and seal up the tunnel entrance. When I get back I'll lock up and hide the key. Who knows if we'll ever be able to operate this brewery again. Those damn Revenuers are breathing down our necks after they arrested Lewis and Fred Buchanen. When I was at their trial where they were sentenced to five years in prison for selling bootleg beer, the ATF boys were hanging out there and questioned me about my possible connection to Lewis and Fred. I of course denied any connection, other than Lewis was my son. But they're a pretty suspicious bunch, and I have a feeling they'll be checking us out pretty closely for a while. That's why we're shutting down the operation. It's just not worth it anymore. I don't want anyone else going to jail for selling or making bootleg. I've collected the last of our take on that last run and paid up all the shippers and sellers."

With that, Andrew left through the secret steel door in the well room of the granary with the satchel. Just as he entered the basement, he heard voices outside and the sound of a car engine idling. He knew right away from the sound of the engine, that it was one of those big V8 engines in one of those ATF pursuit cars. He stuck his head back into the brew house door and said to his sons, "The ATF boys are outside. Lock up and bolt the door and stay put until I get back. I'm going to make a run for it with this money, down along the river and hide it somewhere."

With that, Andrew closed the well room door and hurried out the back basement door of the granary and ran down the hill in the darkness, and down along the river bank. The ATF agents entered the main floor of the hog hog kitchen and yelled, asking if anyone was there. Down below in the basement, Joe, Frank and Peter stopped their cementing and quietly waited. Andrew made his way down the river bank to the old brewery bottling plant and entered the basement door. He made his way to the back and grabbed an empty beer case on his way to the back room where the now empty beer storage vat was. He hurriedly stashed all the bundles of cash into the old beer case, along with the paperwork and the key. He took the beer case and stashed it into the empty beer vat and closed it up securely. He hurried out of the basement and made his way quickly to the farmhouse, just as the ATF car was pulling up in front. Two agents came to the door and Andrew answered. They showed him their badges.

"We were just at your hog barn," the lead agent said.

"Yeah, so," Andrew replied, "I saw you drive in."

"We want to ask you a couple of questions about your hog operation."

"My hogs are none of your damn business," Andrew said.

"Well it's not about just the hogs," the agent said, "we noticed that water tank and steam boiler there on the main floor. Looks like it came from a brewery or maybe a still."

"I bought those when you guys closed down the old brewery. Do you want to see my receipt?"

"No, no, that won't be necessary," the agent replied. But why do you need a steam boiler?"

"We have steam lines that run out into the hog barn to keep the feed troughs from freezing in the winter. It gets cold here in Minnesota. Where you guys from, Florida or someplace? Come back next winter and I'll treat you to some nice warm swill."

"Well, we did test your swill that was left in the mixing tank and it checked out okay, no mashing converted sugars."

"Yah, it's just ground oats and barley and water, kinda like oatmeal. Ya want to take a bucket of it home with you for breakfast?"

"Now, don't be a smart ass," the agent replied, "where are your three sons?"

"They're probably over in the cattle barn doing chores. Did you think to look there?"

"Well, no," the agent replied.

"So, now who's the dumb ass," Andrew asked? "Yah know, I'm pretty damn sick and tired of you guys coming, snooping around here every time you don't have anything better to do. I've been very cooperative so far, just letting you waltz in here any old time of day or night. You've been through the old brewery a dozen times so far this year. That building is now personal property you know. So from now on, your little party is over. I don't want to see your ugly faces on my property again, unless you have a warrant. Got it? You just quit harassing me and my family or I'll file charges on you for searching without cause or a warrant. Now good night, get the hell off my property."

As he slammed the door, Anna came over to him and said, "That sounded like a pretty heated discussion. What's going, on Andrew?"

"Oh, those damn Feds. won't leave us alone. I mean just because we live next to a shuttered brewery, they seem to think somehow, that we're still making beer here, especially after Lewis got in trouble for selling bootleg beer up in Moorhead.

"I know," Anna said, "I feel so bad for Lewis and his friend Fred, getting sentenced to five years in prison after the owner of that speak-easy in Moorhead double-crossed them and ratted on them, then testified against them at their trial"

Andrew just hung his head, feeling very guilty, but he couldn't express any of his guilt to Anna, because she knew absolutely nothing about her husband and son's bootleg business. So he just said that he agreed with her that their son Lewis got a really bad deal. As he turned away, he said he was going out to the barn to help their other sons with the chores.

He walked slowly to the barnyard, he was deep in thought and guilt for what had happened. He was extremely grateful to Lewis for not exposing his bootleg operations. Now they would have to turn their focus to the farming operation and try to completely forget about bootlegging. They had made a huge amount of money, but now they wouldn't be able to spend any of it. The ATF would be monitoring their bank accounts, so the money and gold would have to remain hidden, for the foreseeable future.

Later Andrew would draw up a map with clues to where the illegal money and gold was hidden. "Maybe, sometime in the future, or even some future generation would be able to find the loot," he thought.

"All this, just because I wanted to keep on brewing beer, I've brewed beer my entire life. I started back in Sulzbach, Bavaria, Germany, at my dad's brewery. And now this Prohibition thing. What a lot of nonsense. People have been brewing beer for about six thousand years, starting in ancient Babylon and Egypt. Now our government thinks they are going to stop it. They're fools, those damn politicians for listening to those 'do-gooders' temperance crazies. It won't last. There's almost as much booze being made today illegally as there was legal booze before Prohibition. People want their booze and that's all there's to it. People have to make up their own mind if they want to drink or not."

When he got to the farmyard, he went into the granary basement and into the well room and unlocked the steel door and went into the secret brew chamber. Joe, Frank and Peter were just finishing, sealing up the tunnel entrance.

"Good job," he told them, "why don't you boys go over to the cattle barn and get the chores done. I will finish closing everything down and locking up, then I'll feed the hogs"

The Fellerer brothers left as Andrew checked everything over, making sure the water and steam lines were shut down. He double checked everything and then left through the steel door and locked it. He took his copy of the key, and in a very sad and depressed mood, he dropped the key down into the bottom of the well, never to be found and used again. He left through the well room and closed that door securely. Little did he know, although he suspected,

- - - no one would enter the secret brewery chamber for over a hundred years.

REBELLION

At the national level; just after the Eighteenth Amendment's adoption, there was a significant reduction in alcohol consumption among the general public and particularly among low-income groups. However, consumption soon climbed as underworld entrepreneurs began producing "moonshine" alcohol. With the rise of home distilled alcohol, many cases of careless distilling led to the deaths of many citizens. During the prohibition years, upwards of ten thousand deaths can be attributed to wood alcohol poisoning

Likewise, there was an initial reduction in overall crime associated with the effects of alcohol consumption. There were however, significant increases in crimes involved in the production and distribution of illegal alcohol. Those who continued to use and sell the alcoholic beverages, tended to turn to organized criminal syndicates, who were able to take advantage of uneven or corrupted law enforcement and suddenly overwhelmed police forces.

The production, importation, and distribution of alcoholic beverages that were once the province of legitimate business, were now taken over by criminal gangs. These gangs fought each other for market control in violent confrontations, including murder. Major gangsters, such as Omaha's Tom Dennison and Chicago's Al Capone, became very rich with their take of the movement and sale of illegal booze and operation of **"*Speakeasies*"** and were admired locally and nationally. It is said that Al Capone's annual income from his illegal operations exceeded 60 million dollars a year. Enforcement was difficult because the gangs became so rich and powerful they were able to bribe underpaid and understaffed law enforcement officials and pay for expensive and high powered lawyers. The name Elliot Ness and his crew of Federal Agents in pursuit of these outlaws became a household name during the prohibition years.

Many citizens were sympathetic to the bootleggers, and respectable citizens were lured by the romance of the illegal speakeasies, also called **"*blind tigers*"**. The loosening of social morals during the 1920s included popularizing the **"*cocktail*"** and the *"**cocktail party**"* among higher socio-economic groups.

Those inclined to help authorities were often intimidated, even murdered. In several major cities – such as Chicago and Detroit that served as major points of liquor importation, mainly from Canada, which had no prohibition; the gangs wielded significant political power. A Michigan State Police raid on Detroit's Deutschets Haus, a notorious speakeasy once netted the mayor, the sheriff, and the local congressman. This trend in brewing and transportation of bootleg liquor created a domino effect with criminals across the United States. Some gang leaders were stashing liquor months before the Volstead Act was enforced.

The ability to sustain a lucrative business in bootlegging liquor was largely the result of the minimal police surveillance available at the time. It became increasingly apparent that the designers of the Volstead Act, in a rush to get it approved and passed by Congress, had failed to take into account the large scale opposition to the principle of Prohibition. Mr. Wheeler and Senator Volstead had failed to for-see the lengths that a populace would go to, to continue their entrenchment in a social habit;

that even though harmful in certain ways had also provided them a reprieve from the pressures of daily life. They had completely underestimated the effort, in man-power needed to enforce the rules they had designed. There were only 134 agents designated by the Prohibition Unit to cover all of Illinois, Iowa, Minnesota, and parts of Wisconsin. Another issue was that, many local police were sympathetic to the resistance of the Prohibition Laws. Charles Fitzmorris, Chicago's Chief of Police, during the beginning of the Prohibition period stated, "Sixty percent of my police force were in the bootleg business.

The Act called for trials for anyone charged with an alcohol-related offense, but juries often failed to convict. In the state of New York, the first 4000 arrests led to just six convictions and not one jail sentence.

THE DEATH OF AN INDUSTRY

AND IT'S RESURECTION

The nation's immense brewing industry ground to a halt on January 15, 1920, precisely at midnight, as the 18th Amendment went into effect. Some breweries would survive by producing a very low alcoholic beverage called "near-beer". Near beer was created by brewing regular beer and just before packaging; the beer was re-boiled to evaporate the alcohol.

As with all of the U.S. breweries, the Minnesota breweries were significantly impacted, Many of them, such as the Keiwel Brewery in Little Falls, accommodated a variety of new enterprises while keeping their plants ready to convert back into beer making if the 18th Amendment were to be repealed. Kiewel used its former cold beer cellars to churn and keep ice cream. They also made legal, non-alcoholic beverages.

Some breweries would survive by producing other non-alcoholic products. Some would hang onto the hope of a repeal of the 18th Amendment and keep their breweries intact.

Others however, would never again make beer; as their financial structure and the building structures simply crumbled away as the years of the Great Prohibition wore on.

Unemployment became rampant as the hundreds of thousands of brewery winery and distillery workers, along with the nation's liquor sales, distribution, transportation and saloon workers became unemployed, virtually overnight. There was not yet unemployment benefits in the 1920's. Some believe this streak of large-scale unemployment carried through into the Great Depression. The broad scope of this economic upheaval cannot be underestimated. Its ripple effect would be felt for generations, and can still be seen today. One of the stipulations of the Volstead Act was that breweries were forbidden from owning bars and saloons. Even yet today, breweries can only sell beer to wholesalers.

* * * The Numbers * *

Minnesota breweries numbered about 250 before Prohibition. Only about 25 survived and reopened their doors after Prohibition, and the numbers kept declining for the next 50 years.

(These numbers were extracted from the United States Brewers Association, 1979 Brewers Almanac; Washington DC: 12-13.)

In the year 1875, there were 2783 known breweries operating in the U.S. They produced about 9.5 million barrels of beer annually, with the average production of each brewery at 3,414 barrels annually. (A barrel equals 32 gallons).

In the year 1915, just before Prohibition, the number of breweries had dropped to 1,345. They produced about 59.8 million barrels of beer annually, with the average production of each brewery at 44,461 barrels annually. The per capita annual consumption was at 20 gallons.

In the year 1934, the year after the repeal of Prohibition, the number of breweries was at 756. They produced about 37.7 million barrels of beer annually, with the average production of each brewery at 49,867. The per capita annual consumption was at 7.9 gallons.

In 1980, just before the advent of the "craft breweries," the number of breweries in the U.S. was at 101. They produced about 188.4 million barrels of beer annually, with the average production of each brewery at 1.86 million barrels. Although, the giants, like Anheuser-Busch, and Pabst had production figures of about 90 million annual barrels each. The per capita annual consumption had risen back up to 23.1 gallons.

(One gallon = 128 ounces, or approx. 10 of the 12 oz. cans or bottles). This equates to about 40 six-packs per year, per person.

* * * * **The Rubber Effect** * * * *

As you can see; by 1980, the personal, annual consumption of beer had returned to where it was before Prohibition and even slightly higher at 23.1 gallons per person, per year.

The industry had come full circle in its recovery. The dynamics of the industry itself had changed, but not the end result, which was the personal consumption of beer.

While there were many factors that accounted for this; probably the main overriding factor was the mass-marketing of the product. With the advent of Television, beer commercials were brought right into the living rooms of every American household.

DEATH OF THE BREWERY

1920

On January 16, 1920 Prohibition began. The Volstead Act shut down the brewery at Perham. Andrew Fellerer purchased the brewery buildings from the Perham Holding Company and attempted to produce a non-alcoholic 'near-beer' for about a year, but it never caught on and The Perham Holding Company which still owned the brewery equipment, had to sell off all the equipment to pay off debts incurred by Peter Schroeder as a result of the forced closure of a great many of Minnesota breweries in 1915. So Andrew was no longer employed as the Brew Master of the brewery.

Much of the brewery building was demolished in the process of removing the brewing equipment. The 3 story Brew House and Bottling Plant building however were not demolished; being of sturdy brick, concrete and steel beam construction. During the course of the next 13 years of the Prohibition, the Brew House was used by the Fellerer Farm as a grain storage facility.

Sadly though, even when Prohibition was ended in 1933, the brewery would never again make beer. (But don't tell that to Joe and his dad. They would continue to have a dream of one day re-starting the brewery.)

* * * * * *

Andrew and his sons then turned their attention to the farm. Andrew recommended that he and his sons form a corporation for the managing of the farm, consisting of Andrew and his four sons, Joe, Frank, Louis, and Harry. The name of this corporation was called; The Fellerer Farms Incorporated.

The farm again prospered in the 1920's under this new structure, as more expansion took place. More land was acquired and they now had about 400 acres under cultivation. They increased the livestock herd and a herd of sheep was added. Joe increased his hog operation they built a new hog barn with an automated feeding system. Joe also acquired a grain mill, to mill or grind the grain for hog feed.

Joe's brothers began growing more corn to feed the expanding hog herd. Back in those earlier years, farmers didn't buy their seed corn, there was not yet a 'hi-bred' seed corn. They captured their own seed by selecting the largest ears from the crop, and drying them thoroughly by hanging each ear by its husks on a series of rails across the granary room ceiling, over the winter. In the spring, these ears were run through the corn shelling machine which stripped the kernels from the cobs. These kernels were then ready for planting.

The seed grain for the grain crops was created in similar fashion. Grain was selected from the best field, and then kept in a special 'seed' bin until spring. In the spring this seed grain was 'cleaned'. It was run through a hand cranked machine with a blower fan, and shaker screens that filtered out the weed seeds, and the seed grain was now ready to plant.

There were some good years and some not so good, as was always the case with farming. These were the 'dust bowl' years and clouds of dust rose up from the prairie hilltops. Some years in the dry spring weather, the wind would blow away the soil from around the seeds and then blow away the seeds themselves. Joe and his brothers would try to plant, especially the small grains, oats, barley or wheat right after, or sometimes during a rain when the soil was wet and hopefully the grain would sprout and take root before it could be blown away.

Andrew retired from the farm and put Joe in charge of the corporation. Under Joe's leadership prosperity continued in spite of the dust bowl years and the great depression.   The new prosperity allowed for modernization of the farm. In the 1920's and early1930's, a new John Deere tractor was purchased to replace the old steam engine and a new Chevy truck was purchased to improve and speed up getting grains and livestock to market.

* * * *

As the Prohibition years ground on and on, through the 1920s and into the early 1930s, the old Perham brewery buildings, meantime, stood in shambles; as the Volstead Act had left them, after the Holding Company destroyed much of the buildings when they removed and sold off all the brewing equipment to clear the debts.   The Brew House building remained in-tact however, and was used as a grain storage facility by the Fellerer farm for the duration of Prohibition. The adjacent bottling plant was left intact and later became the home of Joe Fellerer and his family as he attempted to rebuild the brewery.

THE END OF
THE NOBLE EXPERIMENT

THE 21ST AMENDMENT

THE REPEAL OF THE 18TH

1933

Prohibition lost advocates as ignoring the law gained increasing social acceptance and as organized crime violence increased.

In 1932, wealthy industrialist John D Rockefeller, Jr. stated in a published letter:

"When Prohibition was introduced; I hoped that it would be widely supported by public opinion and the day would soon come when the evil effects of alcohol would be recognized. I have slowly and reluctantly came to believe that this has not been the result. Instead, drinking has generally increased; the 'speakeasy' has replaced the saloon, a vast army of lawbreakers has appeared; many of our best citizens have openly ignored Prohibition; respect for the law has been greatly lessened; and crime has increased to a level never seen before".

By 1933, public opposition to prohibition had become overwhelming. In March of that year with the pressure from President Roosevelt, because of his campaign promise to repeal the eighteenth Amendment, Congress first passed the Cullen-Harrison Act, which legalized "3.2 beer" (i.e., beer containing 3.2% alcohol by weight) and wines of similarly low alcoholic content, rather than the 0.5% limit defined by the original Volstead Act.

After more than ten years of the country going dry; on December 6, 1932, Senator John Blaine of Wisconsin submitted a resolution onto the floor of the Senate to submit the Twenty-First Amendment to the states for ratification.

On February, 20, 1933 Congress passed the Blaine Act, a proposed constitutional amendment to repeal the Eighteenth Amendment. When ratified by thirty six states, this would become the Twenty First Amendment to the Constitution of the United States.

The text of the Twenty First Amendment:

Section 1. The eighteenth article of the amendment to the Constitution of the United States is hereby repealed.

Section 2. The transportation or importation into any State, Territory, or possession of the United States for delivery or use therein of intoxicating liquors, in violation of the laws thereof, is hereby prohibited.

Section 3. This article shall be inoperative unless it shall have been ratified as an amendment to the Constitution by conventions in the several States, as provided in the Constitution, within seven years from the date of the submission hereof to the States by the Congress.

Although the U.S. Constitution provides two methods for ratifying constitutional amendments, only one method had been used up until that time; and that was for ratification by the state legislatures of three-fourths of the states.

However, the wisdom of the day was that the lawmakers of many states were either beholden to or simply fearful of the Temperance Lobby. For that reason, when Congress formally proposed the repeal of Prohibition on February 20, 1933 (with the requisite two-thirds having voted in favor in each house; 63 to 21 in the United States Senate and 289 to 121 in the United States House of Representatives), it chose the second ratification method established by Article V, that being via state conventions.

The Twenty First Amendment is the only constitutional amendment ratified by state conventions rather than by the state legislatures. It is the only amendment to have been ratified by state ratifying conventions, specially selected for this purpose. All other amendments have been ratified by state legislatures.

The 21st Amendment is also the only amendment that was ever approved for the explicit purpose of repealing a previously existing amendment to the Constitution.

The first state to ratify the Twenty-first Amendment was Michigan, on April 10, 1933. Minnesota was number 26, on October 10, 1933. Utah was number 36, on December 5, 1933, thus completing the required 36 state ratifications

The amendment was subsequently ratified by; Maine, December 6, 1933 and Montana, August 6, 1934.

The Twenty-first Amendment ending national Prohibition became officially effective on December 15, 1933.

The amendment was rejected by South Carolina, on December 4, 1933,

Voters in that state rejected even holding a convention to consider the amendment: North Carolina did the same on November 7, 1933.

The following states took "No" action to consider the amendment: Georgia, Kansas, Louisiana, Mississippi, Nebraska, North Dakota, Oklahoma, and South Dakota.

The second section of the amendment bans the importation of alcohol in violation of state or territorial law. This has been interpreted to give states essentially; absolute control over alcoholic beverages, and many U.S states still remained "dry" (with state prohibition of alcohol) long after its ratification of the 21st amendment. Mississippi was the last, state still remaining dry until 1966. Kansas continued to prohibit public bars until 1987. Many states, today, delegate the authority over alcohol granted to them by this amendment to their municipalities or counties, (or both).

THE DREAM BEGINS

1933

With Prohibition ending in 1933, and with the additional income from a much expanded farming operation; Joe and his dad began planning in earnest, their dream of restarting their brewery.   Andrew recommended that Joe gain some new experience with the brewing business.   Joe then left the farm and secured a position at the Alexandria brewery in Alexandria, Minnesota, in about 1933.

His first position was that of Cellar Manager, where he learned and performed the job of the fermentation and ageing of the beer. After gaining the knowledge and experience of this phase of the brewing process he then transferred into the Brew House where he learned the mashing and brewing process.

In 1935, Joe learned of the death of his mother, Anna. Anna was dead at the age of 67 from an apparent heart attack. She was Andrew's beloved wife and the mother of their 14 Fellerer children. .

Joe returned to work at the Alexandria brewery. Soon he was promoted to Brew Master of the brewery. As such he was also in charge of the bottling, kegging and selling of the beer to wholesalers in the area. It was in this capacity that he would experience an event that would change his life forever.

It was about 1935, and as he traveled around the Alexandria area selling beer, part of his job was to keep up with beer permits and tax stamps. This of course took him to the Alexandria Court House.

It was here that he met the Clerk of Courts, an attractive young lady named Alice.

ALICE

Alice attended the Alexandria High School, and graduated in 1927. She then graduated from the Fergus Falls Business School, in the town of Fergus Falls, Minnesota, specializing in Court Reporting. She returned to Alexandria where she secured a job as the Clerk of Courts, for Douglas County.

It was in the summer of 1935, that this quite handsome, debonair, middle-age man came into the Douglas County Courthouse to renew his beer selling license. His somewhat suave, yet down-to-earth mannerism struck Alice as the kind of guy she would like to get know better. And he thought she was quite attractive, so he asked her out to dinner.

Joe must have been making good money at the brewery, because he then bought himself a new 1936 Ford Coup with a 'rumble seat'. A very classy car in the 1930's. He was probably trying to impress his new lady friend.

Joe and Alice began dating and soon visited Alice's parents, Martz and Juliana, in the town of Millerville, for dinner.

After they had dinner, Joe and Martz sat on the front porch and were enjoying a cigar and a bottle of Joe's Alexandria beer. They began discussing the beer business. Joe mentioned the Fellerer brewery at Perham, and he and his dad's plans to some-day reopen that brewery. Martz issued his future son-in-law a warning, "I would proceed with caution on that endeavor Joe. A lot of these local small town breweries that are reopening after prohibition are struggling with having old and outdated equipment, after sitting dormant for thirteen years."

"I know," Joe replied, "It's a struggle to keep the Alexandria brewery updated."

"Not only that," Martz continued, "the big breweries in the cities have powerful financial backing and very aggressive marketing and advertising, and are seeking to expand into a much broader market area."

"I can't argue with that," Joe stated, "But I still believe that a small local brewery can succeed, if they can offer a quality product and keep the cost of producing it down."

"Well, I wish you all the luck in the world," Martz replied, "Juliana and I will support you with your plans" A short time later Joe and Alice took a trip to the farm and brewery at Perham to meet Joe's dad, Andrew and his brothers and several of his sisters. At this point in time, almost all of Joe's sisters were already married, and had families. His brothers though, were not, and oddly, would never be.

At the farm Joe took Alice on a tour of the farm, and gave her a history of the development and growth, of the farm over the years. She was very impressed, "This farm is huge," she commented.

"Well, keep in mind that it is a family owned corporate farm, and there were five of us who built it from the original forty acres that Dad and Mom started with, and now we have nearly a thousand acres, and the brewery, of course." They next toured the brewery, or what remained of it after the Prohibition People ripped it apart and removed all of the equipment. "So all that remains here was just a shell of the building," Alice commented. "Boy, oh boy, Joe, it would take a lot of work, and money to restore it and make it operational again."

"Well," Joe replied, "It's been done twice before, and could be done again." And he explained to her, the history of the brewery. As they were leaving to head home, Alice took one last look at the brewery, and had a sudden very strange, albeit faint feeling of home deep inside her subconscious. But little did she actually know that she would soon be spending the rest of her life, living in that brewery.

Joe and Alice dated for just about two years and were married at the Catholic church in Alexandria on June 16, 1937.

However, shortly after the wedding, the Alexandria Brewery closed. The newlywed couple then moved to St. Cloud where Joe took a position at the St. Cloud Brewery as the Bottling Plant Manager.

However within about a year the St. Cloud Brewery closed. This left Joe with two choices; he was offered a job at the Yorg Brewery in St. Paul, or he could return to the farm at Perham. He and Alice began discussing his options. "Well," Joe said, "on the one hand, the job offer at the Yorg Brewery would pay quite well. And with my background, I could probably move up to Brew Master eventually. On the other hand, it would take some getting used-to, working and living in a big city. What do you think, Alice?"

"Well", Alice replied, "I would not mind moving back to St. Paul. After all, my Mom and Dad have put their farm up for sale, and will be moving back to St. Paul because of my Dad's health; along with my sisters Margret, and Louella. But let's be honest Joe, I don't think you would be happy in St. Paul. You have this dream of rebuilding the brewery at Perham, and having your own brewery. That's all you've talked about ever since I met you."

"I'll have to agree with you, there, Honey, that always has been my Dad's and my dream. And besides, I have a feeling that the York brewery is not going to survive very long. When I was there for the interview, I noticed the brewery looked very outdated, and they have very tough competition from the Hamm's and Schmidt breweries."

"I know," Alice said, "I have a feeling that this would be yet another brewery that would close, and leave you hanging. I think the idea of rebuilding the Fellerer brewery would be a better plan. Your family already owns it and you would have a lot of help from your Dad with restarting it, because he worked there and ran it for 30 years before prohibition closed it."

After talking it over with his dad and brothers he decided to return to the farm and pursue the dream of restarting the brewery at Perham, now the Fellerer Brewery.

LIFE IN THE BREWERY

A NEW FAMILY

A NEW GENERATION

In 1939, Joe had to prepare a living place for his new family on the farm. He renovated the Bottling Plant at the brewery with an apartment for his new family. Joe designed the refurbished bottling house with a three bedroom apartment.

Joe then returned to work on the farm, to his hog raising operation. That, along with the beef and sheep and cash crop operations that were run by his brothers Frank, Louis and Henry, were to supply the necessary funding for the reconstruction of the brewery. Joe in the meantime, worked on drawing up the blueprints for the rebuilding of that part of the main section of the brewery that had been torn down at the time that Prohibition shut it down, and the holding company removed all of the brewing equipment.

The newer three story Brew House was not torn down, nor was the Bottling Plant. Because they were both newer and built with steel beams and reinforced floors.

ANOTHER WAR

1940's

Just as Joe and his brothers were about to begin the reconstruction of the brewery, there was that 'Pearl Harbor' thing, and the world was again plunged into yet another World War. So the re-construction was put on hold and Joe and his brothers focused on the farming operation.

At the beginning of the war years the Fellerer family members who were living on the farm included; Andrew, Gretchen, Frank, Louis, Henry and Rose, all of whom lived in the former Brew Masters House on the hill to the left of the brewery. Then there were Joe, Alice and their two sons, Joseph and Robert who lived in the brewery itself, in the former bottling plant.

Prior to the war, Joe had been able to procure some of the equipment for the brewery. He bought a large steam boiler for heat and power to the Brew House, and also a steam engine to power the grain elevator to move the malt to the crushing mill and up to the mashing floor.

Also at this time Joe's brothers; when they were not farming, such as in the winter months, would cut timber for the rebuild. The Fellerer Farms Corporation also owned about 100 acres of pine timber north of White Pine Lake. These acres contained a number of large 'old-growth' trees. These logs were so large that the saw mill could hardly saw them. The Fellerer truck could only haul three logs at a time. Some were in excess of 48 inches in diameter, and the saw blade was only 40 inches. Logs also were harvested from their wooded acreage near the town of Richville, and were hauled to the Fellerer's saw mill on the farm where they were sawed into lumber in the spring and summer months of the early and mid, 1940s.

No building took place yet because of the war. As the war raged on, rationing was imposed on the entire country. Stamps were issued for each commodity under rationing, these were mailed out monthly. You had to request the stamps that you would need for each commodity, and submit a stamp for each item in order to purchase it. Food items such as sugar and flour were under rationing, as well as gasoline and oil and tires. Certain metals were also rationed as well as parts for cars. No new cars were made during the war. But because farming was considered a 'war critical', industry, the rationing was more liberal for farmers. Parts to repair farm equipment were not rationed, nor were tires however they were hard to come by. The farm tractor was fitted with steel wheels with steel cleats. Gasoline and oil were easier to obtain for farmers, but it helped that the Fellerer farm as with many other farms at that time used horses for a great part of their farming. They still kept two or three teams working throughout the war years and beyond.

Finally in 1945 the war ended and rationing was lifted. Also this meant that the re-building of the brewery could get started. More logs were hauled in to the sawmill and sawed. Gravel was also hauled in from a gravel pit at the White Pine Lake woods for the cement work,

THE BREWERY RE-BUILD

By 1946 building began in earnest. First, forms were built and cement was poured to build up the walls that had been torn down. With the construction beginning, Joe was busy scouring the country looking for equipment for the brewery. He found what he wanted in the Wisconsin breweries that had closed. He found the biggest cache at the Monroe brewery in Monroe Wisconsin where he got the mash tub, the brew kettle, hot and cold water tanks, the hot wort tank, eight wooden fermenting tanks, and three steel finishing tanks. At the Gettleman Brewery in Milwaukee he got 90 wooden kegs, the keg washer, the keg filler and two large lager tanks. In the town of Bloomer, Wisconsin, he got the bottle filler, pasteurizer, a bottle labeler, three pressure tanks and the beer filter and filter washer. The large steel tanks were then lowered into the cellars.

Next, more forms were built and the floors were poured. Then more forms and the upper walls were poured. Joe was in charge of all the construction and he was responsible for laying all the brick work on the front of the building.

In 1948, the death of Joe's brother Frank temporarily halted construction. Frank died from complications from pneumonia at the age of 58. He had no children and had never been married. Frank's death was a real blow to Joe. He and Frank were very close and had worked closely together for all those years as they built their farm.

When work resumed, the upper floors were built. First wood 8 X 8 wooden posts were installed, and 8 X 8 wooden beams were added. Then in 1949, the upper flooring was installed.

Work on the building continued through about 1952 with the laying of the roof. The rest of the brewing equipment was hauled in from Wisconsin and installed, as well as the plumbing and sewer system. During the later phases of the construction Joe's three older sons, Joseph, Robert and John became more involved in helping with the building as well as beginning to help with a lot of the farm work, especially chores. Feeding the large livestock herd was one of the many responsibilities.. About five or six dairy cows were added to the two or three already in the herd, and the boys began doing the hand milking. Joe continued to manage the hog operation. Farming continued all through the re-building of the brewery.

In the fall of 1952, Joe saw the death of his father, Andrew, at age 92. Andrew was the true immigrant pioneer, who left his family and country, Germany, and came to America to find a new life in the great American wilderness. Here he braved all the elements of the raw wilderness, the bitter cold and snows of the winters, and the floods of spring, the threat of the unsettled Indian population, the hot and dry droughts of summer, the pestilence of the grasshoppers eating up his farm crops, the remoteness and loneliness of pioneers living in this remote wilderness, the total absence of any of the conveniences of city life. Here he struggled with communicating with other pioneers from practically every country and language of Europe, until one day they all learned one common language, English. He came here to America with just the clothes that he packed with, and started to build a life with no tools or money, just the knowledge that he brought with him, and his love of brewing beer, and his determination to make a living and build and provide for a family. He did an amazing job of managing two separate jobs at once; that of the Brew Master at the brewery, and with his son Joe, managing and building a very large and successful farm.   Andrew never lived to see his beloved brewery operational again. This brewery that he loved and worked at and managed as Brew Master for all of his career, from about 1880 thru 1920 when Prohibition closed the brewery forever. He was preceded in death by his wife Anna in 1935 and his son Frank. His death left his other seven daughters. His sons, Henry and Louis, and daughter Kathrine on the farm as well as his son Joe and his wife Alice and their children; Joseph, Robert, John, Marlene, and James who lived in the brewery.

THE PHOENIX THAT JUST WOULD NOT RISE

Joe and his brothers were determined in 1953 and 1954 to make the now almost completed brewery operational. The building was 95% done, they just needed to put a roof on the old malt dry kiln and get it ready to be a malt storage building equipped with a malt elevator that would transport the malt over to the Brew House. The equipment was about 80% ready. They had begun testing several of the equipment pieces.

They fired up the boiler and tested the steam engine. They water tested all the water and beer lines, and the water and beer tanks, brew kettle and mash tub.

All that was needed was working capital. Joe figured that it would require about $25,000 to get the brewery operational and provide enough working capital to brew beer and begin selling it. Joe and his brothers didn't think that the farm profits would generate enough capital for the start-up money. They figured the only way was to secure a loan, however they didn't want to mortgage the farm. They had formed a corporation, The Fellerer Brewing Company but couldn't get the backing to sell enough stock.

Joe then began applying for loans at several banks and investment companies. The Perham State Bank turned him down because they wanted $10,000 cash reserve, but advised him to apply for a federal loan with the Federal Reconstruction Finance Corp. a small business, government loan. However, (there's that 'However' again), Joe was turned down again because this was 1953 and there was another war going on, the Korean War. They said that the brewing industry was not critical to the war effort. (Come on now, you can't tell me beer isn't critical to a soldier's wellbeing).

After all those attempts at financing, Joe was becoming discouraged, but still hopeful that maybe the farm could provide enough profit for the brewery start-up money. But as the years wore on, it seemed less and less likely that it was going to happen. In the 1950's farm prices were not good and operating costs kept going up. Joe and brothers tried to increase the farm output. They were short-handed without Frank and Andrew but Joe's sons; Joseph, Robert and John were old enough now to provide a lot of the manpower needed for the expansion. They rented more acres and contracted share-cropping to increase the acreage. They purchased more equipment and more tractors to farm the almost 1000 acres they now had under cultivation which in addition to their own farm included four other farms that they were share-cropping

THE SETTING SUN

Finally by 1956 to 1960 there were signs in the western sky above the Perham Prairie, and above the Fellerer farm and brewery. Just as the late afternoon sky begins to fade from its bright blue, into a hint of grey, sometimes just a hint of a paler yellow-orange appears, and if there are those wispy bands of high clouds the sun begins to light them up as if on fire. As the sun sinks farther into the western sky, it produces brilliant shades of orange and red-orange. Then as the sun appears through an opening between the clouds and the western horizon it lights up the entire sky with a spectacular display of those blazing red-orange colors, as if the sun is melting and the liquid sun is pouring out upon the earth like molten metal, spreading across the entire world. A final good-by from the sun until it appears again.

And so, the sun was setting on the 'Fellerer Empire', on this pioneer family, on the Fellerer farm and brewery, and on Joe Fellerer's life story.

In 1956 thru 1960, Joe became totally discouraged about ever restarting the brewery when his three oldest sons left home, Joseph and John to college and Robert to the Army, and then college. After the older boys left, Joe's youngest son James began helping with the farm work, doing milking and field work with Joe's brother Louis. But with the shortage of manpower, the farming was greatly diminished. There had been just no way to get the financing necessary to get the brewery back into production. Joe and his brothers were just too old by this time to make it happen.

THE END GAME

1960 - 1980's

So in 1968, Joe and his brother Louis made a deal with the Land-O-Lakes Company to sell them the farm land. The Land-O-Lakes Company wanted the farm land to build a treatment system for the waste water from their cheese processing plant in Perham. Some very contentious discussions took place between Joe and Louis about whether or not to sell the farmyard and brewery along with the farmland. The Land-O-Lakes Company didn't 'need' the farmyard and brewery for the waste water disposal. They wanted it to protect their polluting of the underground aquifer water from being discovered. Joe, was 81 years old, and wanted to keep the farmyard and brewery to hand down to his heirs.

Louis wanted to get rid of it all. He said he was "fed up with all of it." He maintained a very disgruntled attitude about the whole concept of restoring and re-opening the brewery, and was herd saying, "I don't want to spend the rest of my life scrubbing out beer tanks." In the end, apparently Louis won out and made the deal. Under this deal the Fellerer's would keep the homestead and brewery until they both passed, but the Land-O-Lakes Company had an option to buy it and refused to negotiate a sell-back to Joe Fellerer's family.

This was the story of their brewery on the banks of the beautiful Ottertail River and how the Great Prohibition of the 1920's closed down their brewery forever.

THE END

EPILOGUE

And so, after living on this farm and brewery for 100 years, the Fellerer family decided to sell their legacy, and regrettably did not pass it on to the next generation.

As for the Fellerer brewery; at Perham; after prohibition closed it in 1920, the brewery never again made beer. When Prohibition ended in 1933, Joe Fellerer and his father, Andrew, and brothers worked for twenty years trying to restore it, but, were unable to come up with the financing to complete the renovation and bring the brewery into production. Sadly, the window of opportunity for them closed as they became too old to complete the job.

As for the brewery and farm, they no longer exist, - - - - - in the physical world. They exist now, only in our memories, and in the pages of this story.

The brewery was completely torn down in 1986 by the Land-O-Lakes Company and lies buried forever beneath the banks of the beautiful Ottertail River.

ACKNOWLEDGEMENTS

I would first like to express my thanks to my beautiful wife Barbara for all the love and support, and the patience she has given me in this endeavor. She has been such a phenomenal help with the spelling and grammar, and the multiple proof readings.

Thanks to our daughter Brenda for proofreading the multiple versions and additions to the story.

Thanks to our dear sister Marlene, for her help and encouragement, and contributions to the project.

Thanks to brothers Joseph, John, and Jim for allowing me to tap their brains for additional historical information and memories.

Thanks also to the History Museum of East Ottertail County in Perham, Minnesota, for their help with providing the background history of the Perham area.

A special thanks to Zachery and Colby Fellerer; the great-great grandsons of Andrew and Anna Fellerer, for inspiring me to write these books and help build the diorama of the Fellerer farm and brewery, which now resides in the East Ottertail County museum.

If you're ever in the town of Perham, Minnesota; stop in at the East Ottertail County Museum and view the diorama of the Fellerer farm and brewery.

If you enjoyed the story of the **GREAT PROHIBITION** and how it impacted the Fellerer family brewery,

Look for other exciting new books by author:
ROBB FELDER

* * * * * * * *

Go to www.otterfallspublishing.com
to see more background about all of the books in the OTTER FALLS SERIES:
PIONEERS ON THE OTTERTAIL
MYSTERY ON THE OTTERTAIL
ADVENTURES ON THE OTTERTAIL
RETURN TO OTTER FALLS

Take a look at the new releases by; **ROBB FELDER**

LAST FLIGHT OF THE SNOWBIRDS'

THE COLD COLD WAR
And

PROHIBITION THE NOBLE EXPERIMENT

ABOUT THE AUTHOR

ROBB FELDER Is a Vietnam Veteran. He attended the University of Alaska and the University of Minnesota. He grew up in the brewery and on the farm talked about in the story. He is the author of the **OTTER FALLS SERIES. THE LAST FLIGHT OF THE SNOWBIRDS and THE COLD COLD WAR.** Robb is retired from a successful career as a computer applications software designer. He and his wife Barbara live in a suburb of the Twin Cities of Minnesota.

211

www.ingramcontent.com/pod-product-compliance
Lightning Source LLC
Chambersburg PA
CBHW070503120726
47910CB00003B/1112